# Ancrene Riwle

## Introduction and Part I

# medieval & renaissance texts & studies

## Volume 31

# Ancrene Riwle

## Introduction and Part I

EDITED AND TRANSLATED

WITH COMMENTARY

BY

## Robert W. Ackerman

AND

## Roger Dahood

medieval & renaissance texts & studies

Binghamton, New York

1984

A grant from the University of Arizona Research
Foundation has aided in meeting production costs.

**Library of Congress Cataloging in Publication Data**

Ancren riwle. Introduction.
  Ancrene riwle.

  (Medieval & Renaissance texts & studies; v. 31)
  Includes the Middle English text from the Manuscript Cotton Cleopatra C.IV of the
British Library.
  Bibliography:
  1. Monasticism and religious orders for women — — Rules.   2. Monastic and religious
life of women — — History — — Middle Ages, 600-1500 — — Sources.   I. Ackerman,
Robert William, 1910-1980.   II. Dahood, Roger, 1942-      III. Ancren riwle. Part
1.   1984.   IV. Title.   V. Series.

PR1808.A25   1984                     255'.901                     83-21987
ISBN 0-866898-055-5

Printed in the United States of America

# Contents

*To*

*Gretchen P. Ackerman*

# Preface

The Introduction and Part I of *Ancrene Riwle* (from the text of British Library MS Cotton Cleopatra C.VI) are here newly edited with a facing-page translation. The General Introduction and explanatory notes, mainly the work of Professor Ackerman, were largely in final form before his death in 1980. In readying the book for press I have made revisions and additions in the notes, all nonetheless within what I conceive to have been the scope of his intention, and all, I hope, such as he would have approved. I have indicated my responsibility for substantive changes by placing my initials (R.D.) in round brackets at appropriate places. The General Introduction includes a brief history of medieval anchorites and a discussion of the anchoress's daily prayers, the subject of Part I of the treatise. Professor Ackerman deliberately refrained from detailed analysis of the liturgical traditions drawn upon in Part I. It was his belief, however, that such analysis by a competent liturgical scholar might well lead to the identification of service books close in form and content to the exemplar from which the sister anchoresses copied their office (see Part I, note 27).

The text and translation are my contribution to the edition. I have transcribed the text from a microfilm copy supplied by the British Library and checked it against the manuscript.

Professor Ackerman would have wished to acknowledge the generous counsel and assistance of Father Fabian Parmisano, O.P., in the task of identifying the medieval texts of the numerous prayers, hymns, antiphons, supplementary offices, and devotions referred to in Part I. He would also have gratefully acknowledged the valuable advice of Professors William Storey and George H. Brown.

My thanks are due to T. F. Hoad for reading a draft of the edition. Many of his suggestions are incorporated into the final version. I wish also to thank Nancy Mairs, Charles Chamberlain, and Carl Berkhout.

I am happy to acknowledge the many courtesies extended to Professor Ackerman and me by the staff of the British Library and, in particular, of the Department of Manuscripts. Grants to Professor Ackerman from the American Council of Learned Societies and the American Philosophical Society enabled him to conduct necessary research in England. And it is a pleasure to record a generous grant from the University of Arizona Foundation toward the cost of publication.

ROGER DAHOOD

*Tucson*
*October* 1982

# General Introduction

# General Introduction

The aim of the present edition is to make available for students an often neglected portion of *Ancrene Riwle* in a form demonstrably close to that which was actually known and used in the thirteenth century. These pages set forth, in addition to the short Introduction, the daily round of devotions, the central core of the anchoress's existence. In his edition, restricted to Parts VI and VII, Geoffrey Shepherd was particularly interested in those moving passages designed, in his words, "to stimulate and control acts of penance and love in daily life."[1] Our chief concern is with the prescribed program of worship, which in our opinion supplies the proper context for understanding the spiritual and domestic advice in the remainder of the treatise.

In view of the intense study of *AR* over the years, it is surprising that the elaborate prescriptions for the anchoress's liturgical day given in Part I have not long since been better explicated. Modern secularism and a consequent failure to understand a life of prayer and renunciation may explain why commentators and literary historians seem inclined to pass over Part I, as they do the Introduction, with *pro forma* remarks.[2] In fact, students of Middle English, whose acquaintance with *AR* is all too likely to be limited to anthologized extracts, are allowed to gain the impression that this is the composition of a kindly old cleric, mildly concerned lest his anchoresses keep more than one cat or indulge in gossip or painful mortification of the flesh, a man often given to quoting the Bible, St. Augustine, and St. Gregory, spinning out moral allegories about the sow of gluttony, and enlivening his rule by humorous references to Slurry the cook's boy.[3] In actuality, as will be made clear, he bound the anchoresses to a relatively severe regimen.

## The Manuscripts and Early Scholarship

*AR* first came to be known to readers other than a very few students of manuscripts only in 1853, with the publication of the Reverend James Morton's edition and translation,[4] and only after some decades was it recognized as a work of superior literary merit. It came to be especially esteemed because of its direct and charming rendering of the author's mind and individuality and also as an important monument of early Middle English, or "semi-Saxon," to use Morton's term.[5] During the past fifty years, few works in Middle English have been more painstakingly investigated. The imagery and other stylistic aspects of the author's prose have been analyzed,[6] and the sources — scriptural, patristic, and otherwise — have been searched out. There have also been many attempts to identify the author, his ecclesiastical status or monastic order, the three sister anchoresses for whom he composed his rule, and the location of their anchorhold.[7] Other studies have dealt with the structure, the later revisions, and the wide circulation of the work in medieval times.[8]

A large segment of *AR* scholarship has concerned the interrelationship of the eighteen manuscripts and fragments now known and the date and original language of composition. For the rule is extant in Latin, French, and Middle English versions.[9] Close examination of all forms of the work has resulted in general endorsement of Morton's opinion that *AR* was composed in English, although arguments have been made for Latin and French as the original languages.[10] Morton's opinion is borne out by Professor E. J. Dobson's work on manuscript affiliations. Dobson also has developed a strong case for dating the composition between 1215 and 1222 and for regarding MS Cotton Cleopatra C.VI as providing possibly our earliest copy, since it appears to have been written between 1225 and 1230.[11] The basic language of *AR*, called the "AB dialect" by J. R. R. Tolkien, is widely agreed to be that of Hereford, that is, the English of the Southwest Midlands.[12]

In an effort to provide a text generally faithful to a form of *AR* almost certainly used in the thirteenth century for the purpose intended by the author, that is, for the governance of anchoritic life, we have relied on the version in MS Cotton Cleopatra C.VI. This manuscript is notable not only because of its early date, mentioned above, but also because it bears physical evidence, far more than any other copy extant, of use over several decades. The evidence in question is the heavy emendation in four hands of varying dates appearing especially on a very high proportion of the first nineteen folios of the copy.[13] It is by no means unreasonable to envisage this small, plump volume in the hands of a long succession of English anchorites and their spiritual directors. Only in terms of conscientious study by many such as these can one explain the countless interlinear and marginal revisions: corrections of spelling, punctuation, and syntax, supplying of subheads and other aids to ready reference, extension of quotations, addition of new matter, and rephrasing intended to clarify the sense.

The plethora of revisions, some of them corrections of corrections, makes for hard reading. Indeed, only one who has pored over the cluttered manuscript pages is able to appreciate Dobson's achievement in producing his edition of the Cleopatra version, without which any serious use of this text would be far more difficult.

In his commentary, Dobson provides a sophisticated analysis of the revisions. Thus, he observes that the whole of the Cleopatra version was copied by a single, less than reliable scribe, designated as "A," and that A occasionally went back to correct a few of his own mistakes. He concludes that the French translation preserved in the fourteenth-century MS Cotton Vitellius F.VII[14] is derived from the exemplar used by copyist A of Cleopatra and at times is a superior rendering of that exemplar. Most of the alterations in Cleopatra, however, are in two other hands, one early and the other distinctly later. Dobson holds that the earlier corrector, called "B," emended A's text possibly within a year or two of its completion, that is, between 1225 and 1230. B not only corrected errors left by A, but he introduced material that would adapt the rule to the needs of an already enlarged community of anchoresses. Dobson argues further that the character of B's changes and also his dialect, belonging to Hereford, as A's dialect does not, suggest that he was none other than the author of *AR*, an interesting but scarcely necessary conclusion.[15]

Dobson considers MS Corpus Christi College, Cambridge, 402,[16] of a date close to that of Cleopatra, to be a fair copy of the rule as revised by B and also the most nearly "correct" version available to us. Nevertheless, the A copy in Cleopatra seems occasionally, if in a minor way, to offer a better reading than Corpus, as in the rehearsal of the contents of *AR* at the end of the Introduction. The third "distinction," or part, as A accurately informs us (Cleopatra, fol. 8v), consists of likening the anchoress to five kinds of birds. But Corpus, in agreement with the other manuscripts of *AR*, speaks of *anes cunnes fuheles*, "birds of one kind," to which David, as an anchorite, compared himself. In fact, Part III of the rule goes beyond the biblical basis for this comparison (Psalm 101.6-7), for in the Psalm only three different birds are mentioned. Moreover, the margins of Cleopatra contain emendations by B not carried over into Corpus which nonetheless improve the sense of the basic text. An example occurring on the first folio of *AR* in Cleopatra (fol. 4r) is furnished by B's altogether appropriate comment about conscience.

The later of the two chief revisers of Cleopatra, "D," seems to have worked toward the close of the thirteenth century. His revisions, which Dobson characterizes as foolish meddling, consist mainly of adding Latin subheads, altering punctuation marks, inserting Latin glosses above English words, and sometimes falsifying the original by these and other changes.[17]

As editors of the Introduction and Part I, we are primarily concerned with only the first nineteen folios of the Cleopatra text, yet these few leaves contain literally hundreds of revisions in the hands of B and D, as may be seen in Dobson's apparatus. The present edition is not simply a transcription of the basic work of copyist A. Because of our interest in offering a consistent text as it would seem to have been read by thirteenth-century anchoresses and others relying on the Cleopatra MS, we have incorporated into our text most of the corrections and additions supplied by B. In thus modifying the rule as first written by A, we have tried to include only those revisions which contribute to intelligibility and grammatical integrity, at all times keeping in mind what is known from other sources about anchoritic life. Although we have consulted both the Corpus version and the French translation, mentioned above, we do not always accede to their authority in adopting or rejecting revisions in Cleopatra. All liberties taken with A's text are acknowledged in the notes. The headnote preceding the text and translation explains our policy in such matters in greater detail.

## The Medieval Anchorite

*AR* sets out a way of life for which no clear modern parallel exists, although today certain monastic orders, such as the Camaldolese and Carthusians, make provision for members to lead at least a semi-eremitical life. Thus, a brief survey of what is known about medieval anchorites and their background is a desirable prelude to a discussion of *AR*. Also to be clarified is the relationship which the anchorites bore to other professed religious men and women—that is, the hermit, monk, and nun.

Late Latin *anachorita, anchorita, anchoreta* (Eccles. Gr. ἀναχωρητής, "one who retires from the world") passed into English as *ancra* around the year 1000.[18] The common-gender form *ancre* appears in Middle English, the specifically feminine *anchoress* not being recorded until the end of the fourteenth century.[19] Modern English *anchorite* (or *anchoret*) functions both as a generic term and a masculine.[20] But the etymological meaning, "one who retires from the world," is of virtually no use in setting the anchorite apart from other kinds of religious. For the word *hermit* (Gr. ἐρημίτης, "a desert dweller") conveys the same general meaning as does *monk* (Gr. μοναχός adj., "solitary"). All three terms were applied more or less indiscriminately to the Desert Fathers, who in the third century began in some numbers to take up a solitary life of self-denial and meditation in the wilderness of the Thebaïd, or northern Egypt. Apparently the worldliness that overtook many Christians when the persecutions ceased during the reign of Constantine was responsible for the flow of religiously motivated men and women to the desert. These fugitives were primarily laymen, although a few early hermits ultimately entered the priesthood. The reputation for holiness acquired by some as the result of their miracles of faith-healing, exorcism, and prophecy attracted to their remote huts and caves in Egypt and various places in the Near East hordes of the pious in search of edification and help. From such petitioners, communities of people dedicated to the religious life grew up both in wilderness areas, around the now often violated retreats of the masters, and in cities, such as Alexandria. Some of these were loose agglomerations of hermit cells, but others developed into organized communities promoting a common religious life. For the governance of the integrated communities, the early rules ascribed to St. Pachomius (d. ca. 348) and St. Basil the Great (d. 379) were composed. Somewhat illogically, the expression *monastery*, "a place for dwelling alone," was applied to such new congregations, and the term *monk* designated a male member of the group. A more accurate word than *monk* also emerged — namely, *cenobite* (Lat. *coenobita*, Gr. κοινόβιος, "common life").[21]

Meanwhile, persons known as anchorites or hermits continued to take up a solitary life, although such writers as Cassian (d. ca. 435) quite early perceived dangers associated with passing from the world into absolute isolation. Lone dwellers in the wilderness were not only subject to harassment by outlaws; they were likely to be distracted from prayer and meditation by the constant need for providing food and shelter for themselves. Moreover, pride in the arduous life and also self-indulgence were spiritual or psychological pitfalls for one completely separated from human contacts for long periods. For such reasons, even the early authorities came to favor less than total isolation. Beyond that, later authorities held that ordinary men should not undertake the eremitical life before undergoing the discipline of the cloister.[22]

Whether hermits or cenobites, the religious of the first Christian centuries pursued a program of prayer and meditation, of work, manual or literary, and of austere self-denial. Separation from society in the interests of cultivating a higher level of self-knowledge was recommended by ancient philosophers, including Pythagoras and Plato; and among pre-Christian Jews, sects such as the Essenes lived a severely segregated existence. Types of the monastic profession were found in the scriptural accounts of Samuel, Elijah, and St. John the Baptist, although Christ was regarded as the true founder of religious life. Commonly cited in this connection was Christ's forty days' sojourn in the wilderness. Among the most illustrious of the Egyptian Fathers, St. Paul, called the first hermit (d. 342), was said to have received bread from ravens just as had Elijah (1 Kings 17:4). St. Ammon (d. ca. 350), who dwelt for years with his wife in brotherly chastity, was credited with numerous miracles. St. Anthony (d. 356), after many decades as a solitary, founded a monastery reputed to have been the first. He further assisted St. Ammon in organizing a monastery for his disciples, who had been dwelling in scattered hermit cells. Two Desert Fathers of the same name, St. Macarius the Elder (d. 390) and St. Macarius of Alexandria (d. 394), likewise spent most of their lives in isolation, although both served as spiritual parents to many admirers, and accepted priest's orders.[23] The author of *AR*, it may be noted, names Paul, Anthony, and one of the Macariuses in his Introduction, along with other famed exemplars of religious life.

Not content with the discomforts and dangers of a harsh, largely unpopulated region, of crude dwelling places, and of the minimum of food, clothing, and shelter, the early religious, strongly influenced by the cult of martyrs that grew up in the deserts of Egypt, commonly inflicted corporal punishment on themselves. They devised ingenious tortures, including not only prodigal fasting but remaining in a standing or kneeling posture for incredible periods, wearing hair shirts or coats of mail, and scourging with thorns. The Syrian monk, St. Simeon the Stylite (d. 459), early in his career wore a tight rope around his waist, causing the flesh to fester. It was later said that this most famous of the "stationaries" mounted a succession of pillars, standing thereon for the last thirty-seven years of his life and preaching to the crowds of the pious and curious below him. Thus, mortification of the flesh, and especially flagellation and the hair shirt, became a part of religious life. St. Peter Damian, the eleventh-century Cardinal-Bishop of Ostia and a Benedictine monk, strongly endorsed discipline, administered publicly or privately, either by the individual himself or by a benevolent hand. He believed that the blows of the whip made a sound as agreeable to God as the tympanum of the psalmist. St. Francis of Assisi likewise recommended this form of mortification to his friars. To medieval Christians in general, self-torture seemed altogether fitting and meritorious, not merely for the sake of taming the bodily appetites, but more importantly because only through actual pain would one become sufficiently mindful of the agonies of Christ's passion.[24]

Religious life in all its forms was soon transmitted from the East to Rome and the West. The saints and doctors of the Church figured importantly in spreading abroad a knowledge and appreciation of the hermits and cenobites of the East. Included are St. Athanasius, Archbishop of Constantinople (d. 373), who brought two Egyptian monks with him to Rome during one of his periods of exile; St. Jerome (d. 420), who wrote much of his Vulgate Bible in a monastery in Bethlehem; and St. Augustine (d. 430), who is credited with having organized a small community of religious in Hippo. By the time that St. Benedict (480–547) as a very young man encountered at Subiaco the humble monk who assisted him in taking up the eremitical life, many religious houses and many solitaries were to be found in Italy and some to the north in Gaul. During the last calamitous days of the Western Empire, these institutions and individuals did something to mitigate the savagery of the barbarian invaders.[25]

The great rule which St. Benedict wrote after he had left his hermitage to establish several cenobitical communities, most notably Monte Cassino, not only superseded the rule of St. Basil, heretofore used in the West, but became the model for many other rules. The *Benedictine Rule*, it should be noted here, opens with a classification of the types of "monks" known to the saint: (1) *cenobites*, or monks proper, who lived in a community under a rule; (2) *anchorites*, that is to say, hermits ("deinde secundum genus est anchoritarum, id est hermitarum"), who after long probation in a monastery were deemed fit to venture into the world to fight the devil; (3) *sarabites*, who lived in small groups subject to no rule; and (4) *gyrovagi*, or wanderers, who fell readily into sin, being without stability. For St. Benedict, the anchorite was still identical to the hermit, but he believed that the cloister was the proper novitiate of the anchorite. That he should align monks with hermits or anchorites in this fashion is scarcely surprising in view of the fact that, like the Desert Fathers, he was himself a hermit before becoming a monk and abbot. Moreover, he seems always to have cherished a hope of someday returning to the solitary life. Mature observation of many religious charlatans obviously underlies his contempt for sarabites and gyrovagi.[26]

The solitary ideal, the nearly total renunciation of the world of men as well as of property, continued to exert a powerful appeal. But the term *hermit* came in time to be restricted, more or less consistently, to solitaries who, shunning a fixed abode, were free to wander about or to dwell in remote regions. Some, to be sure, inhabited cells near religious houses, and other fugitives from society dwelt near forest roads or isolated bridges which they maintained as a work of charity.[27] A liturgical office for the institution of hermits came into being, and rules governing their conduct of life were composed, even though no *regula eremitarum* regarded as standard seems ever to have emerged during the Middle Ages.[28] As readers of the Arthurian legend know, hermit-priests figure in medieval literature; nevertheless, such historical records as we possess suggest that relatively few hermits were ordained priests. Moreover, the number of men who became hermits only after the period of monastic discipline recommended by St. Benedict and St. Peter Damian was probably small. In fact, many must have assumed the status of hermit altogether without ecclesiastical sanction. The great English mystic Richard Rolle of Hampole (ca. 1300–1340) bowed to no such conventions when he took up the eremitical life clad in garments borrowed from his father and sisters. For every Richard Rolle, there must always have been numerous vagabonds, as mentioned by St. Benedict, who affected bare feet and unkempt appearance in order to further their true vocation as beggars — "in habite of an hermite unholy of werkes," to quote Langland.[29]

A parallel specialization of meaning ultimately overtook *anchorite*, which came to be reserved for those solitaries, the recluses, committed by their vows to constancy of abode, normally a cramped cell. Some forms of reclusion were adopted by early Desert Fathers, such as St. Anthony, who immured himself for a term of twenty years. Such an inmate, of course, was obliged to depend on those outside for the necessities of life, and it was therefore natural that the place of enclosure should be within or near a religious community and that many recluses should themselves be monks and nuns. As early as 692 the Council of Trullo passed legislation specifically dealing with monks who would be anchorites. Further, formal licensing by the abbot and an episcopal benediction were required. Conventual recluses, both men and women, were known in the West at an early date, as Gregory of Tours (ca. 538–593) testifies.[30] Reclusion was certainly practiced in England, and there by the thirteenth century the person called an anchorite was more likely to be an enclosed solitary than a hermit, as is strongly suggested in a doctrinal treatise, *Vices and Virtues* (ca. 1200): "Ðese twa lif, hermit and ansæte [withdrawn] lif, ðe we nu clepeð anker."[31]

It is, of course, with non-conventual anchorites, or more specifically anchoresses, that *AR* is concerned. The anchoritic life, in contrast to the exposed existence of the usual hermit, was well-suited to women, a fact that explains the large number, if not the preponderance, of female solitaries, at least in England. Furthermore, the anchorite's stability of abode assured that he lived under closer ecclesiastical control than did the hermit. Perhaps for this reason, the anchorite was generally regarded as having chosen an especially arduous form of religious dedication.[32]

Although the earliest anchorites were not provided with a manual for their guidance, rules for recluses eventually came into being, some intended for conventual recluses and later ones for those not living under monastic supervision. Of these, Grimlaic's *Rule of Solitaries* (*Regula Solitariorum*), composed in a Bavarian monastery in about 900 for the governance of male recluses, is particularly instructive. The monk who felt a vocation for a more completely meditative life than was possible in the choir, refectory, and dormitory with his brethren was advised by Grimlaic first to petition his abbot and apparently also the bishop for enclosure. If adjudged sufficiently sincere and stable by his superiors, he would be allowed to live apart from his community in solitude for a probationary year. The permission of abbot or bishop and even the blessing of his fellow monks had to be secured if he wished to persevere. Only after successfully completing these steps would he be ceremoniously conducted to a cell where his enclosure was symbolized by the bishop's seal. Grimlaic indicates that proximity to the chapel would permit the inmate to hear the choir services. Recluses in priest's orders were to have their own altars for the celebration of Mass, and all were to recite the Divine Office in their cells. A fenced garden was to be available, and since the dangers of absolute and long-continued solitude were recognized, limited speech with recluses in nearby cells was permitted. Provision was also made for those who attracted disciples to offer spiritual counsel through a window. Nevertheless, the business proper to the anchorite consisted of solitary worship, meditation, and reading, relieved only by occasional work with the hands.[33]

Two centuries later, Goscelin of Wilton (d. ca. 1100), a French Benedictine who lived most of his life in English abbeys, wrote his *Liber Confortorius* (ca. 1080) for Ève, a young woman whom he regarded as his spiritual daughter. After a long period in the royal monastery of Wilton, Ève went to Angers and entered an establishment housing several recluses. Rather than a rule, Goscelin's *Liber* is an epistle dealing in broad terms with the secluded life. Ève's cell may be narrow, he writes, but is not the whole world a prison? Again, since the cell serves at once as oratory, refectory, and dormitory, is it not equal to a palace? Moreover, even though she dwells in a sepulchre, as it were, Ève must remember that the resurrection took place in a grave. Goscelin's remarks on the daily regime are sparse. Ève should divide her time between prayer and reading. Her prayer is to be centered on the monastic hours, during which she should bear in mind the suffering of Christ and the conception of the Virgin. Goscelin further recommends his own practice of reciting five psalms (Pss. 21-25) in memory of the five wounds of Christ.[34]

The work of Goscelin stands somewhat to one side of the main tradition, but another epistle addressed to a female recluse—namely, St. Ailred of Rievaulx's *On Regulations for Recluses (De Institutis Inclusarum)*—exerted considerable influence and was quoted by the author of *AR*. The distinguished St. Ailred (1100-1167) was abbot of the Cistercian house at Rievaulx in Yorkshire for the last twenty years of his life, and he was also the author of spiritual works and valued counselor of King David of Scotland. Among his other responsibilities, he found time to write a lengthy rule for recluses at the behest of an older sister, evidently a religious who had embraced the solitary life. Ailred took much of his material for this rule from Benedict, Jerome, Cassian, Ambrose, Augustine, and Gregory, although in his two final chapters he dwells on his own youthful concupiscence as contrasted with the steady virtue of his sister. He exhorts her to practice the contemplative life typified by Mary, to shun the company of others, to avoid teaching the young, and to maintain silence so that her meditations might be the more intense and fruitful. That she was to recite the Divine Office and devotions to the Virgin Mary is made clear in three chapters in particular, and she was further to have prayers always in her mind while working with her hands and throughout the rest of each day.[35]

Yet another Latin rule, *The Rule of the Recluses of Dublin (Regula Reclusorum Dublinensis)*, may appropriately be mentioned here despite the fact that it was composed at a time somewhat later than *AR*, to which it may well be directly indebted. Moreover, the Dublin treatise, although intended for both men and women, also shows affinities to St. Ailred's rule.[36] The Dublin rule counsels moderation in such austerities as fasting and tends to discuss the anchorite's inner life more fully than does St. Ailred. Moreover, its author is fond of extended metaphor and word play, even though in such respects he is no match for the author of *AR*. For example, the recluse is advised to eat his daily bread with the teeth of the mind, for in this way he will grow in wisdom and spiritual beauty. The precepts of God, sweet to the soul but bitter to the body, teach us to be oblivious to the temptations of gluttony and all worldly solaces. Further, the word *anchorite*, because of its alleged etymological

identification with the anchor of a ship, is made to yield edifying
significance. Daily Mass at the third hour is recommended, and
the anchorite is to take communion each Sunday, much more frequently than stipulated in *AR*. He should further, like the monk,
recite matins and all the hours, not all of them together in the manner of secular priests, but at their established times. Also, he should
praise the Blessed Mary and include in his devotions the Seven
Penitential Psalms and, on the anniversaries of benefactors, prayers.
Beyond this, prayer should always be in his mouth and heart, and
all work should be accomplished in humility. Like the hermit of
the desert, the anchorite should live in silence; upon his enclosure
he should regard himself as dead to the world.[37]

Further attention to the rules just mentioned is reserved for the
discussion that follows. The present historical overview, however,
would be incomplete without some remarks about English anchorites
and an attempt to visualize the sister anchoresses of *AR* in context.

Diocesan and other records yield allusions to individuals who
took up the solitary life both within and without monastic houses
as early as the seventh century. Historians have tabulated a large
number of such references in twelfth- and thirteenth-century records.
The number is much greater in the fourteenth century, but it then
dwindles to nearly nothing by the first part of the sixteenth. Conventual recluses, both men and women, dwelt in such Benedictine
abbeys and priories as Crowland, Durham, and Westminster, and
also in Augustinian, Franciscan, Carmelite, and Dominican friaries.
Further, cells for solitaries were to be found in St. Giles in Hereford
and other hospitals, and in castles, including Dover, as adjuncts
to chapels. Many English anchorites were enclosed in cells adjoin-
ing parish churches, and we have notices of anchorages on main
thoroughfares and by well-traveled bridges. Within the church at
Chester-le-Street, Durham, are the most complete known architectural remains of a medieval anchorage, a two-storied apartment
with a "squint" in the upper chamber permitting a direct view of
the high altar. Perhaps more typical were huts built "under the eaves"
on the north side of the church, as at Hartlip, Kent. Vestiges of
suspected anchorages have been found at various other parish
churches, such as All Saints, York, and at Leatherhead and Comp-
ton in Surrey.[38]

Several anchorites of record were celebrated for saintliness. St.
Guthlac (d. 714), whose *vita* was turned into Old English, was the

first Englishman to achieve fame by retiring from the world in the manner of the Desert Fathers. For many years, he lived as a penitent on an uninhabited island in Lincolnshire under the most primitive conditions, combating the temptations and monsters sent by the devil. The popularly canonized St. Wulfric of Haselbury, Somerset (d. 1159), had been a priest with an unseemly passion for hunting and hawking. Converted by a chance conversation with a beggar, he had himself immured in a cell attached to the church at Haselbury, and there he subjected himself to harsh discipline, wearing a chain cuirass next to his skin and reciting the entire Psalter every night while immersed in a tub of cold water. The early twelfth-century recluses of Kilburn, who were once proposed as the original sisters for whom *AR* was written, should also be remembered in this connection. Two noblewomen of the thirteenth century, Lauretta, Countess of Leicester, and Katherine of Ledbury, Lady Audley, became anchoresses after they were widowed. Wordsworth made the pious legend concerning the latter of these ladies the subject of his sonnet, "St. Catherine of Ledbury."[39] In the late fourteenth century, Walter Hilton (d. 1396) wrote his *Scale of Perfection* for nuns who had entered seclusion. Much moral counsel is included in this book, but it differs from the earlier rules because Hilton's ultimate purpose was to foster the state of mystic ecstasy. A younger contemporary, Juliana of Norwich, was a recluse whose *Revelations* describe a series of heaven-sent visions.[40]

In the first decades of the thirteenth century when an anonymous ecclesiastic composed *AR* for the guidance of three ladies in religious seclusion somewhere in Hereford, the anchoritic life was clearly an established tradition. Yet neither at this time nor later were anchorites sufficiently numerous to become as familiar a part of the religious landscape of medieval England as were members of the regular orders of monks and, later, friars. To be sure, the layfolk in a number of parishes supported and very possibly took considerable pride in having an anchorite in their churchyard, and still other solitaries dwelt in cells equally visible to all. The remainder, the conventual recluses, were sequestered from the public. Anchorites, then, must have represented a very small proportion of the totality of men and women in the service of religion at any one time.[41] The records suggest that at least a slight majority of anchorites were women, and further that in England a significant number were priests, monks, friars, or nuns at the time of their enclosure. By no means did those who entered an anchorage as members of religious orders necessarily become recluses in monastic precincts, for we find more than a few inmates of churchyard cells designated in historical documents as monks and nuns. On the other hand, it is reasonable to suppose that monastic *reclusaria* housed only professed members of the order. That many anchorites entered their cells as laymen rather than as religious, and were thus devoid of monastic experience, is certain. Unlike Ailred's sister, the ladies for whom *AR* was written were in this category. But whatever their previous status, those who aspired to the anchoritic life seem, more consistently than hermits, to have placed themselves under the guidance of a qualified spiritual director and to have submitted to a solemn rite of enclosure. If the office signalizing the enclosure of the three sisters of *AR* resembled that preserved in Bishop Lacy's *Pontifical*, it involved Extreme Unction, the sprinkling of dust, and the sealing of the doorway to the living tomb.[42]

The physical surroundings of the three sister anchoresses for whom *AR* was originally written emerge rather distinctly in the rule. One gathers that each woman was committed to one of several rooms built onto a church, presumably along one side of the nave. The individual quarters were large enough to accommodate the anchoress and her indoor maidservant; other servants, it is suggested, went about the neighborhood begging food for the inmates. The anchoresses were permitted to communicate with the others' maidservants at interior windows in the partition walls. Each cell was also equipped with a window or "squint" opening into the church and permitting a view of the high altar. Still another window, the smallest of all, opened into the churchyard or street, but this one was to be kept heavily curtained. The furniture must have been of the meagerest, but the religious objects were rather numerous, consisting of a holy water stoup, a crucifix, possibly in addition a larger cross with or without the *corpus*, and as many as two or three altars before images of the Virgin and of other saints. The altars, one or more of which might be consecrated to permit a private celebration of Mass, were also used to hold saints' relics for veneration.[43] Personal belongings were confined to a few articles of coarse clothing, table ware, sewing equipment, liturgical texts, and a few other edifying books, probably in English and French.

## *Abstract of Ancrene Riwle*

A sound understanding of the Introduction and Part I, on which
the present study is focused, requires some attention to the relationship or contribution of these opening pages to the whole of *AR*.
An abstract of the rule, necessarily selective, will be useful in this
connection. For ease of reference, the inclusive folio numbers of
the Cleopatra manuscript are given at the head of each separate
part, together with the corresponding page numbers in Dobson's
edition. It should be admitted at the outset that no abstract or
abridgment of a work so rich in imagery, allusion, and allegory
can convey an adequate notion of the original.

**Introduction** [Fols. 4–9; Dobson, pp. 1–15]
Two rules govern religious life. The inner or "lady" rule concerns the heart, which must be kept "right" in its quest for God.
As the commandment of God, this rule in invariable. The outer
rule, the "handmaid," pertains to the body and exterior life. Its
primary function is to serve the inner rule. Because it is man-made,
it is less rigid and fixed than the inner rule and should vary according to the individual's age, strength, degree of learning, and the like.
The anchoress should make no more than three solemn vows,
which may be violated only on pain of mortal sin: obedience to
a bishop or other superior, chastity, and stability of abode. Charity, observance of the Ten Commandments, confession, penitence,
and the like are decreed by God.
She should say that she belongs to the order of St. James if any
inquire as to her religious profession. In his epistle (1:27), James
bids us succor widows and children and keep ourselves uncon-
taminated by the world. The first part applies to the good religious
who live in the world; the second particularly to the anchoress. For
a solitary, true religion does not inhere in the color of the habit,
whether black or white. In religious communities, however, the
wearing of the same habit symbolizes inward unity. Micah (6:8)
tells us to walk with God.
The parts or "distinctions" of *AR* are enumerated as follows: I.
Devotions; II. The Five Senses; III. David's Comparison of Himself
to Birds of the Psalter; IV. Fleshly and Spiritual Temptations; V.
Confession; VI. Penance; VII. Cleanness of Heart and the Love
of Christ; and VIII. The Outer Rule.

## I. Devotions[44] [Fols. 9–19v; Dobson, pp. 15–38]

Upon awakening, the anchoress should cross herself, say *in nomine Patris, Veni, Creator spiritus* and other devotions, and then while dressing recite the *Pater Noster* and the Creed. She should thereafter continue with meditation on the crucified Christ, recite prayers in memory of the five wounds, and venerate the relics on each of her altars.

She then may begin the Matins of Our Lady, prefacing it with a *Pater Noster* and the Nicene Creed. In reciting the Matins and other hours of Our Lady, the differences between week-days and feasts must be observed and also the differences between the summer and winter calendar. Attention is also called to periods of silence and to the fact that, whereas two meals a day are allowed in summer, only one is allowed in winter except on Sunday.

In addition to the Hours of Our Lady, the following supplementary devotions must be said: *Preciosa*, which follows the hour of prime; *Placebo*, or Vespers of the Office of the Dead; *Dirige*, or Matins and Lauds of the Office of the Dead; Suffrages, or prayers to the Trinity, the cross, and the saints, or for the souls of the departed; Commendations, or the commending of the souls of the dead to God; the Litany of the Saints; the Seven Penitential Psalms; the Fifteen Gradual Psalms; and additional prayers and supplications.

The anchoress may recite English prayers for her private devotions, such as an English paraphrase of the *Pater Noster* and prayers to the five wounds, to the seven gifts of the Holy Spirit, to the Ten Commandments, and to the Twelve Apostles. Other devotions will serve, apparently as suffrages and for private use: prayers, to the saints the anchoress most loves, for those who have performed the six works of mercy, for the souls of those who believed in the Gospels, and for the sick and sorrowful.

At the elevation of the Host in Mass, the anchoress should say a series of prayers, and at the kiss of peace, she should forget all the world and extend her love to the Savior.

At midday, she should meditate on the cross, uttering specified prayers. Thereafter, she should pray to Our Lady, using five English prayers and devotions.

Finally, the anchoress should heed a number of miscellaneous instructions and recommendations. She should include in her daily devotions the Office of the Holy Ghost, if she wishes. Moreover, she should kneel before and after meals, read from the Psalter in French or English, avoid idleness, listen to the priest's hours when possible, say graces at meals, and the like. Whoever does not know the hours may say instead a stipulated number of *Pater Nosters* and *Aves*, and concessions are granted to those who are ill.

## II. The Five Senses [Fols. 19v–48; Dobson, pp. 39–94]

The heart is the life of the soul, but it is also a wild creature which must be guarded. Its guardians are the five senses. The eyes are windows which should be curtained in black with crosses on both sides. Lucifer, when he looked upon himself, leapt into pride. The story of David and Bathsheba provides an example of the sins of the eyes. The anchoress should keep her parlor window closed, refusing to open it for any man and rarely for a woman. Speech, the second sense, belongs to the mouth. The anchoress should not set herself up as learned when replying to her priest, nor should she give counsel to a man unless she is of advanced age. Remembering that Eve talked too much to the adder, the anchoress must not emulate the cackling hen. She should not converse at her church window through which she sees the Blessed Sacrament. Silence is to be maintained at meals, and guests must be entertained by servants. Our Lady, who spoke seldom, ought to be the ideal for all women. The ears, the organs of the third sense, should be stopped against all idle and evil talk. The anchoress should be wary of backbiters and the three kinds of flatterers. The sins of the eyes, mouth, and ears are all treated in Scripture and by the Fathers, such as St. Gregory.

Smell, the fourth sense, may be deceitful, for the devil can make something good smell bad and can conceal evil under a ravishing fragrance. A genuinely holy smell appeals to the heart more than to the nose. Holy water and the sign of the cross will help one avoid deceptions. Christ, hanging on Mount Calvary, was surrounded by the stench of decaying bodies. He suffered particularly in the senses of touch and feeling and also in taste when offered the drink of gall. Moreover, he felt inward anguish as if of wounds made by three spears. One was the weeping of his mother and the other Marys, the second was the desertion of the Disciples, and the third was the grief that he had in his heart for the sinfulness of those who put him to death. Christ was wounded in five places because his blood is to be understood as healing mankind of the sins of the

five senses. His perfect steadfastness is a reminder, especially to
anchoresses, that the life of the soul may be preserved only by proper custody of the senses.

### III. David's Comparison of Himself to Birds in the Psalter [Fols. 48–74; Dobson, pp. 94–135]

Not only must the heart be protected by control of the five senses,
but it must grow in humility. The anchoress should remember the
pelican of David's psalm (101:7), for this bird, said to slay her own
young out of anger, is an image of wrath. The anchoress should
guard herself against becoming provoked by another's hateful
speech, for words are no more than air. The remedy for wrath arising from such speech is a sense of joy in the opportunity for forgiving
a transgressor. Because of its thinness and supposed preference for
solitude, the pelican also offers a good example to the anchoress,
as does Judith shut up in her chamber. Because of its austerity,
the pelican is light of weight and can soar into the air, and so should
the anchoress be capable of spiritual flight. Such heavy birds as
the ostrich, on the other hand, are earthbound. The anchoress must
be content with a hard, thorny nest or anchorage, and in her abode
she should place the love of Christ just as the eagle carries the agate
into her nest in order to ward off poison.

The anchoress's attention should further be called to the
nightraven in the same psalm. Just as this bird gathers food by
night, so should the anchoress spend her nights gathering the fruits
of holy contemplation. She should be watchful like the sparrow.
The author gives eight reasons for remaining ever vigilant, including
the brevity of man's life on earth and the sternness of the Judgment. Further, he gives eight reasons for fleeing into solitude, including fear of the devil, who like a mad lion ranges through the
world. He holds up Queen Esther, the Hidden One, as a model
for the life of seclusion.

The anchoress should not only lead a solitary life, as does the
pelican, she should sing her prayers alone in emulation of the lone
sparrow. And she should be mindful that, just as the sparrow is
subject to falling sickness, so she is always subject to temptation.

### IV. Temptations [Fols. 74–135v; Dobson, pp. 135–219]

However holy her life, the anchoress must not think herself immune to temptation, for the higher the hill of holy living, the stronger is the fiend's puff of wind. The anchoress should be wary if she feels no temptation, for, as St. Gregory says, one is then in the greatest peril.

We are prey to two kinds of temptations, the outer and the inner. The former arise from external and internal discomfort and comfort. External discomfort includes illness, shame, misfortune, and every bodily harm. Internal discomfort includes pain of the heart and anger. External comfort includes bodily health, sufficient food, drink, and clothing. Internal comfort includes false happiness of men's praise or of being loved more than another. Patience is the greatest weapon for combating outer temptations, especially those arising from illness. Physical affliction should be looked on as the goldsmith of heaven, gilding one's crown. All the physical pain of this world in comparison with eternal torment is but a game of ball, a drop of dew in comparison to the wide sea. One must remember that those who speak evil of one or do one harm are a file that makes the soul smooth and bright. Every sorrow of this world is of God's sending, a proof of his love for us.

Inner temptations are also twofold, having bodily and spiritual aspects. Here belong the seven capital sins and their vile progeny, for lechery, gluttony, and sloth are bodily in their effects, and pride, envy, wrath, and avarice are spiritual. The flesh incites us to bodily sin, the world urges us to seek prosperity and honor, and the devil leads us into pride, disdain, and the like. In the wilderness through which we must pass, like the children of Israel, we must beware of the many lions of pride, the adder of poisonous envy, the unicorn of wrath, the bear of sloth, the fox of avarice, the sow of gluttony, and the scorpion with tail of stinking lechery. Each one of these has many cubs. Thus the offspring of the lion of pride are named vainglory, scorn, hypocrisy, presumption, disobedience, loquacity, blasphemy, impatience, and willfulness. The progeny of the scorpion of lechery include fornication, adultery, loss of maidenhood, incest, and others too foul to name.

All vices are connected with the seven deadly sins or their offspring. The lion of pride kills all the proud, the adder all the envious, and so with the others. The proud are the trumpeters of the devil, the wrathful man is the devil's knife-thrower, the slothful man sleeps in his bosom, the avaricious man is his fire-tender, and the glutton is his manciple. The lecher by his stink pleases the devil. The anchoress who believes that she will be strongly tempted during only the first year or so of her religious life is in error. In the early years resisting temptation is child's play. A wise husband tolerates unpleasing behavior in a new bride, but once sure of her love chastens her. So Jesus will deal with the anchoress. But at last he will give her joy, just as he gave rest to the children of Israel after long suffering in the wilderness.

Four degrees of temptation may be distinguished, according to whether they are strong or weak, open or concealed. Concealed temptations are especially insidious. Thus the devil can urge a woman on to such extremes of abstinence that her soul will die as the result of bodily suffering. Never trust the noonday devil, as David calls him.

Comforts or remedies are available in the struggle against temptation. For example, an anchoress should remember that she is a tower and that the higher the tower, the stronger the wind. She should bear in mind that the attack on a castle wall will cease only after the castle surrenders. Again, in allowing her to be tempted, God is playing with her just as a mother does with a child. Also, through her resistance the anchoress injures the devil a hundred times more than he can injure her. No one will be saved, says St. Paul, except by struggling against temptation.

Additional medicines include meditation, anguished prayer, reading, fasting, humility, and magnanimity. The anchoress should consider what she would do if suddenly confronted by the devil or if in a crowded church someone were to call *fire! fire!* Such thoughts combat temptation. Moreover, the devil is impaled by prayers flying heavenward just as he is scalded by the hot tears of contrition. An anchoress is a castle and should defend her walls with the moat of humility. With faith, she should laugh the old ape, the devil, to scorn.

The anchoress should consider how the seven deadly sins can be routed by faith. For example, it is not possible to think oneself great if one recalls how small God made Himself in a poor virgin's womb. It is not possible to be wrathful in the face of the threefold peace of God: peace between man and man, God and man, and man and angel. Unlike the foxes in Judges tied tail to tail, the faces of anchoresses should always be lovingly turned towards each other, for the devil is less able to harm those who are thus united. It is not possible to be slothful when one thinks how busy Christ was on earth.

The remedy for pride is humility; for envy, love of fellow-men; for wrath, patience; for sloth, reading, work, and spiritual comfort; for avarice, contempt for worldly things. The body is a foul vessel, food for worms. In the soul are sin and ignorance.

When an anchoress sees the dog of hell slinking toward her with his fleas of stinking thoughts, with crucifix in hand she should order him away and beat him on the back. Whenever she feels the growth of excessive love for worldly things, she should tread on the serpent's head, for much may come from little, from one spark may come a fire.

## V. Confession [Fols. 135v–159v; Dobson, pp. 219–57]

The anchoress should take heed of six powers and sixteen qualities of confession. Among its powers, confession destroys the devil's power by hacking off his head and dispersing his army, as is illustrated in the deed of Judith, meaning "confession," who beheaded Holofernes, a fiend of hell. Again, after the death of Joshua, or "health," in Judges, the Lord appointed Judah, or "confession," as the new leader. Confession restores to us our loss by washing out our sins and making us again children of God.

As for its qualities, confession must be accusatory, bitter with sorrow, whole, naked, frequent, speedy, humble, shamefaced, fearful, and more. With respect to the first quality, the anchoress should not emulate Adam and Eve, who blamed the serpent for their transgression rather than themselves. St. Augustine says that man should ascend the tribunal of his own soul when he considers the Day of Judgment. Reason should be his judge, memory his accuser, and conscience a witness against him. Fear should come forth to bind him so that he might not repeat his sins. Reason should also order sorrow to afflict the heart with sore repentance. Further, bitter confession is a remedy for the seeming sweetness of sin. Confession must be whole, embracing all sins from early childhood. When a poor widow wants to clean her house, she sweeps all the dust into a heap and pushes it out of the house. She repeats the procedure to get all that is left. If her house is very dusty, she next sprinkles water on the smaller particles and sweeps them out. In this way a person should make confession, first pushing out the great sins, then the smaller. If light thoughts blow up like small dust one should sprinkle them with tears, lest they blind the eyes of the heart. A woman will say, "I have been foolish" or "I had a lover," whereas she should confess, "I am a stud mare, a stinking whore."

Six circumstances of a sin must be revealed: any other person involved, place, time, manner, frequency, and cause. Confession should be made often and should follow the act very promptly, for one should not sleep while deadly sin holds a sword over his head. A woman who has lost her needle or a cobbler his awl seeks the lost object at once, turning over every straw. The author lists nine considerations that should hasten confession, including the possibility of sudden death or debilitating illness. Delay is a bad habit. Lazarus stank after only four days in the tomb; how much more the sinful stink after four or five years without confession. Confession must also be humble, like the publican's rather than the Pharisee's. It should also be made in red-faced shame and in fear, yet with hope. Of two millstones, the lower, which bears the heavy load, signifies fear, but the upper stone signifies hope, for it turns and grinds out good works. Likewise, confession should be prudent, truthful, and voluntary; it should deal with one's own sins, be made with the intention of turning from sin, and be well considered.

The anchoresses are instructed to confess sins of pride, haughty heart, envy, wrath, sloth, idle words, gluttony, and excessive abstinence. Also they are to confess if they have said their hours badly. They are to atone at once for minor faults by falling before the altar in the form of a cross and saying *mea culpa*.

## VI. Penance [Fols. 159v–178v; Dobson, pp. 257–81]

Three kinds of God's chosen are on earth: the first may be likened to good pilgrims, the second to the dead, and the third to those hanged voluntarily on the cross of Jesus. The first are good, the second better, and the third the best.

As St. Peter says, good pilgrims travel their course curbing their worldly appetites. The lives of the dead are hidden with Christ. The pilgrims experience troubles but the dead do not since they await resurrection with no concern. He who is on the cross, however, reaps joy and honor as the reward for his shame and torment. The true anchoress is not only a pilgrim and not only dead to the world; she is able to rejoice in having accepted a kind of martyrdom. Shame and torment, as St. Bernard says, are the two uprights of the ladder that reaches to heaven, and the rungs are the virtues by which men climb upwards. Likewise, shame and torment together form the wheels of Elijah's heaven-bound chariot of fire. Life on earth is warfare, as Job says, and we must suffer gladly, for through suffering we come to reign with Christ.

One asks, "What good do I do for God by my torments?" But, as St. Ailred wrote to his sister, one may attain purity only in two ways. One is through mortification of the body by fasting, vigils, discipline, and great labor. The other is through the virtues: devotion, compassion, love, humility, and such. No one can be chaste when pampered with worldly comforts. One should not be too ready to assuage bodily discomforts and illnesses with medicines. It is better to be a free child of God than a healthy thrall to sin. The three Marys brought ointments to Christ, signifying the bitterness of sin, of resisting temptation, and of longing for heaven while still in the world; Mary means "bitterness." But the spices they applied to Christ's body illustrate how sweetness follows bitterness.

The author compares Christ to a recluse. Mary's womb and the stone sepulchre were his anchorholds. And just as Christ went out of his mother's womb and out of the sepulchre, leaving both intact, so the anchoress shall in death emerge from her two anchorholds, her body and her cell, leaving both intact.

The author explains that all he has said about mortification of the body is not intended for the anchoresses since they sometimes afflict themselves more than they should. Yet, just as young trees are encircled with thorns to protect them from beasts, so the anchoresses should guard their purity by undergoing voluntary hardships. They should endure cheerfully the scorn of Slurry the cook's boy.

## VII. Love [Fols. 178v–190v; Dobson, pp. 281–300]

St. Paul bears witness that all physical hardships are as nothing compared with love, which cleanses and brightens the heart. All the bodily agony one can inflict on himself and all the alms he can give are of no avail without love of God and man. Above all things, the author urges the anchoresses to strive for a pure heart, that is, to love or desire nothing but God, and to love others and to esteem things such as food only for the sake of God. God deserves our love, for he gave us the world, and Christ loved the Church and sacrificed his life for it.

The author relates a story of a lady surrounded by foes in her earthen castle. Courted by a king who sent her precious gifts, she

remained indifferent to him. At last he went forth to meet her
enemies and was tormented and slain by them. The author asks
whether the lady would not be evil if she failed to love him after
this sacrifice. The king is Jesus and the lady is the human soul whose
love was sought by Christ. He chose not to deliver the lady from
her enemies by any means other than his own death in order to
reveal the strength of his love.

There are four earthly loves: between friends, between man and
woman, between mother and child, and between body and soul.
But Christ's love for his spouse, the Church, surpasses all four. As
urine, sand, and vinegar quench Greek fire, so sin, idleness, and
a sour heart quench the love of the Lord. Whoever has a sour heart
is a companion of the Jews and is offering vinegar to Christ. The
anchoresses should stretch forth their love to Jesus.

**VIII. The Outer Life**[45] [Fols. 191–198v; Dobson, pp. 301–317]

The anchoresses should receive communion fifteen times a year
on stipulated feast days. In preparation, they should be shriven
and take discipline (but self-administered discipline only). They
should go without their pittance.[46] If they cannot take communion
on a stipulated day, they should take it on the following Sunday.

From Easter until the Feast of the Exaltation of the Holy Cross
(14 September) they are to eat two meals daily except on Fridays,
the Ember Days, and a few others. On those days and during Advent they should eat no white food, except when unavoidable. During the other half of the year, they should fast, Sundays excepted.
Flesh and fat are only for the very weak and ill. The anchoresses
should drink little but are allowed to eat as many vegetables as they
wish. The author remarks that the anchoresses' abstinence from
food and drink has sometimes seemed to him greater than desirable,
and he tells them to fast on bread and water only when they have
leave to do so.

They are forbidden to eat with guests in their anchorage, for
an anchoress ought to be dead to the world. The author observes
that he has often heard that the dead speak with the living but never
that they eat with the living. He instructs the anchoresses to refrain
from entertaining others, from encouraging strangers to visit, and
from distributing others' alms too lavishly. They should play the
quiet part of Mary rather than the part of Martha the housewife.
Even rich anchoresses and those who till a garden should not become

known as openhanded. They may, however, give meals to women and children who come to work for them, but must not, except in real necessity, permit any man to eat in their presence. They should accept what they need from good friends but shun the reputation of "gathering" anchoresses.

They may keep no animal save a cat, for an anchoress who keeps other animals, such as a cow, resembles Martha rather than Mary. They must avoid any business transaction, for the anchoress who engages in trade sells her soul to the merchant of hell. They should not keep other people's possessions in their anchorhold. They should allow no man to sleep there. They should wear plain, warm, well-made garments; whether of white or black is of no consequence. They must wear no linen, save of the coarsest kind, next to their flesh. They must sleep in belted gowns and refrain from donning anything made of iron, hair, or hedgehog skin. They should not beat themselves with a leaded whip or briars or draw blood in taking discipline, except with their confessor's special permission. They need not wear wimples, but in the presence of others should at least wear cap and veil. They are forbidden to wear rings, brooches, or gloves. They are permitted to sew church vestments and clothing for the destitute but not fancy purses to distribute as gifts. They must give nothing away and accept nothing without leave from their confessor. They must avoid idleness, for in idleness temptations are strong.

The anchoresses' maidens may offer instruction to small girls, but the anchoresses should devote themselves to God. They must have their hair cut to lighten their heads, and they may be bled from time to time. They are advised not to overtax their strength for three days after a bloodletting. If an anchoress does not have food ready at hand, she may have two women servants, one to stay always at home, one to go out as needed to purvey food. The servant who goes out should be plainly dressed and say prayers as she goes about. She should avoid gossip.

The anchoresses are to read this last section to their women each week until the women know it. The anchoresses themselves are to read in *AR* much or little every day. The author hopes that it will prove helpful through God's grace, and says that he would rather set out for Rome than undertake to write it again. He counsels the anchoresses to thank God, if they practice what they read; if not, to pray for God's help to follow it better. He prays that the

Father, Son, and Holy Ghost will guard the anchoresses, and concludes with a request that as often as they read from *AR*, they greet Our Lady with an *Ave* for the sake of him who labored over it.

The overall organization or mode of articulation of *AR* is apparent even in the above summary. The distinction between the inner and outer rules announced in the Introduction, for example, is respected with a fair degree of consistency throughout. The author tells us that the first and last parts are devoted to matters of the outer rule, the governance of the body and external life, whereas the six parts separating these two deal with the state of the soul.[47] Allowance must be made, of course, for an occasional overlapping of the two rules, as in the instructions for confession. The opening topic of the inner rule is fittingly enough the control of the five senses, or gateways to the soul, and it is followed in Part III by an exhortation to the anchoresses to meditate on the virtues of the solitary life. The two succeeding parts on temptation and confession seem to return to what may be called the parochial or popular level of discourse marking the discussion of the senses. This is especially true of the disproportionately lengthy, albeit fascinating, allegories of the sins in Part IV. In fact, Parts II, IV, and V may be read as forerunners of the great mass of doctrinal treatises of the later thirteenth and of the fourteenth century.[48] The suggestion has even been advanced that at least Parts IV and V originated as an earlier separate work on confession by the author of *AR*.[49] Part VI appears to be meant more directly for the anchoress, for the penance treated here is the mortification of the flesh as practiced by an ascetic rather than the normal satisfaction required of a penitent by his confessor. The final topic of the central section is an allegorized meditation on divine love, the keynote of which is St. Paul's doctrine of charity.[50]

*AR* departs broadly from earlier rules, including St. Ailred's, which the author knew and quoted. One innovation is the inclusion of more or less popular discourses on the sins and confession mentioned above. A second major departure, the complex devotional instructions making up the whole of Part I, is discussed separately in the following pages. Beyond this, the author was a gifted writer whose work is a joy to read today, not simply because of the often elaborate allegorical embellishment, but also on account of the note of personal warmth he was able to inject. This tone is in strong contrast to St. Benedict's preoccupation throughout much of his rule with administrative matters, and to St. Ailred's aloofness in his epistle to his sister. Only Goscelin's letter to Ève conveys a somewhat comparable suggestion of a warm human relationship.

Such original features of *AR* may suggest a higher degree of independence of earlier rules and the traditions of religious life than in fact exists. Personal solicitude is certainly given a new prominence, yet one should not take the warnings against wearing a shirt of hair or hedgehog skin or lashing the back with a leaded whip too uncritically as a sentiment that bespeaks an especially enlightened, humane cleric. Set against these statements is the casual assumption at the beginning of Part VIII that the anchoress will as a matter of course take discipline at least on the fifteen occasions during the year when she prepares for communion. The anchoress, in fact, is merely advised against over-severe practices. It should be noted, moreover, that admonitions of this sort, although less warmly expressed, appear in earlier rules at least from the time of St. Benedict. Boasts of moderation and disclaimers of undue asceticism tend to occur, in fact, in the very midst of prescriptions for the most uncompromisingly rigorous aspects of religious life.[51]

## *The Anchoress's Devotions*

A brief survey of earlier liturgical practices[52] will indicate the extent to which the regimen of prayer prescribed in Part I of *AR* may be considered traditional.

All rules treat in some fashion the religious worship binding on those to whom they were addressed, in this respect harking back to the great charter of religious life in the West, the *Rule of St. Benedict*. Here, after comments about various types of "monks," observations on the qualifications and paternal authority of the abbot, a list of the seventy-one *instrumenta bonorum,* and homilies on obedience, taciturnity, periods of complete silence, and humility, St. Benedict presents a detailed account of daily prayer. The dozen chapters devoted to this subject constitute the classical formulation of the hours, also referred to as the Divine Office or the monastic hours.[53] Along with attendance at mass[54] and private prayer, the keeping of the hours made up the monk's daily devotions, his *opus*

*Dei*. St. Benedict regarded the *opus Dei* or *opus divinum* as the primary obligation of the monastic day, just as he thought of the monastery as a school of salvation.[55] Yet, as is well known, the monk's daily obligations were tripartite, since in addition he was required to participate in spiritual or theological reading — *lectio divina* — and manual work — *opus manuum* — whether in the fields or elsewhere.

With respect to the hours, St. Benedict systematized and otherwise improved upon the earlier diversity of usages. For he decreed that, during each twenty-four hours, his monks should assemble in choir seven times in the day and once at night, as suggested by the Psalter, "Seven times in the day I gave praise to you," and, "In the middle of the night I rose to praise you" (Ps. 118:164, 62), for performing services consisting basically of psalms, lessons, prayers, hymns, and antiphons. The names given most of the individual hours were derived from the Roman division of the day, and thus they indicate roughly the time of their celebration.[56] The late afternoon office called vespers was commonly considered the beginning of the liturgical day, but here it is less confusing to list the services in the framework of the modern time scheme: (1) matins, also called vigils or nocturns, was said very early in the morning; (2) lauds, in conjunction with or soon after matins; (3) prime, near the first hour of daylight; (4) terce, two hours or so after prime; (5) sext, at about noon; (6) none, early afternoon; (7) vespers, late afternoon; and (8) compline, in the evening immediately before retiring.[57] It is also true that compline differed from the other hours, for in monastic communities the opening parts consisted of readings held normally in the chapter house, after which the monks entered the church for the completion of the office.[58]

Even in the so-called primitive office of the Benedictine rule, the organization of the hours was complicated by several factors. For example, the differences in the periods of daylight and darkness between summer and winter required the devising of an abbreviated night office for summer. Thus, matins for weekdays in summer included only one lesson (selected passages from scripture, the acts of the saints, or the Fathers), whereas in winter three lessons were recited or chanted. Another problem was the distribution throughout the hours of the 150 psalms, to the end that the entire Psalter might be recited each week. Furthermore, the content and in some degree the form of the hours depended on the calendar, whether they were said on weekdays (*feriae*) or on Sundays or feast days.[59] The texts making up the office were for long distributed among several books, including the Psalter, antiphonary, hymnal, lectionary, responsorial, Gospels, and the book of homilies. In the eleventh century, however, we begin to find these elements collected in a single volume, the breviary. Because it was portable, the breviary could be used for private recitation by monks whose duties required their temporary absence from the cloister.[60]

The formalization of daily prayer by the clergy in secular churches was a later development. A full office in emulation of monastic practice seems not to have become general much before the eleventh century, although precursors in the form of a requirement for the celebration of a partial *cursus* may be found in the proceedings of eighth-century councils. But with the appearance of canons regular in cathedral and collegiate churches,[61] a "canonical" office came into use and was celebrated with chant and ceremony much like the monastic office. In content, canonical practice differed somewhat from St. Benedict's prescriptions, principally in the lectionary, or readings. Moreover, customs varied from one diocese to another. The Use of Sarum (Salisbury was one of the "secular" cathedrals) was very widespread in medieval England, but the Uses of York and Hereford were also well known.[62]

Breviaries embodying the canonical offices came to be compiled at an early date, and it is clear that secular clergy, like the monks, were allowed to read their office in private and, when necessary, at times suited to their convenience, even though private recitation was generally regarded as an evil. All secular priests, and not merely those living in community as canons, came under the requirement, and they were to join in the celebration in a church whenever possible. With respect to the extension of the breviary obligation to clerics in minor orders, practice varied during the Middle Ages.[63] In modern times, the requirement came to be more precisely defined.[64]

The addition of votive offices as a result of the growing popularity of the cult of saints enlarged the breviaries. Beginning in the ninth century, in fact, daily prayer, as performed in a number of influential monasteries, acquired accretions, and these tended to multiply and to be adopted more or less universally despite efforts of prelates and councils, especially in the thirteenth century, to limit them.[65] A plausible explanation for this trend is that the segregated monastic life fostered the concept of monks and nuns as a class apart, the *raison d'être* of which was constant intercessory prayer for patrons and, indeed, for all mankind. That is, monasteries were often esteemed not because they offered a means of achieving sanctification but rather because of their presumed value to society. As if in response to such a view, the monastic liturgy became increasingly elaborate and splendid. Following the lead of St. Benedict of Aniane (ca. 745–821), monasteries of the Cluniac congregation, especially in the eleventh and twelfth centuries, adopted extensive additions to the Mass and choir office. The additions to the Divine Office consisted of new observances including the reciting of the Seven Penitential and the Fifteen Gradual Psalms, and also the daily, or at least frequent, performance of new votive offices in honor of the Dead, of All Saints, of Our Lady, and the like. Because they arose as special devotions for morning and evening, the votive offices tended to include no more than matins, lauds, and vespers. The Lady Office is an exception in this respect. Choir duty, particularly in Cluniac houses, preempted a great part of the monk's time and energy, at the expense, of course, of his attention to reading, private prayer, meditation, and manual work. Inevitably, a reaction against the inflated liturgy and also the wealth and magnificence flaunted by many abbeys made itself felt in the formation of new orders dedicated to poverty and austerity. The Cistercians, for example, sought a return to the letter of the Benedictine rule and to this end simplified the liturgy, reinstated manual work, and renounced superfluous ornamentation in their churches. On their part, the austere Carthusians sharply curtailed the monk's choir service in order to free him for prayer and meditation in his cell.[66]

That the elaboration of the monastic liturgy originating on the Continent soon affected English practice may be seen in the famous *Regularis Concordia*, considered on the authority of Aelfric to be the work (ca. 970) of Ethelwold, pupil of St. Dunstan. This treatise, evidently designed to normalize the observances of such abbeys as Glastonbury, Abingdon, and Ramsey, delineates in detail the conduct of the monastic day. The hours as set forth by St. Benedict are taken for granted, but great emphasis is placed on supplementary devotions, including the Penitential Psalms, the Litany, prayers for the king, queen, and benefactors, and the offices of the Dead and of All Saints. The accompanying ceremonial is spelled out, as is the procedure to be followed in chapter, and due attention is paid the summer and winter scheduling of the hours and the masses. Obedience to this elaborate *horarium* must have required the monk to spend at least five hours of each day in choir,[67] although the exigencies of conducting community affairs demanded that excuses be granted rather freely. The parish priest, as already indicated, could fulfill such sacerdotal obligations in a far shorter time, being permitted to read his office silently and at times convenient to him. If the vicar or rector of a parish, however, he might well have been expected to give a public performance of vespers on Saturday, matins on Sunday morning, and possibly vespers again Sunday evening.

That recluses were considered bound to their hours is made clear by the rules reviewed above. Grimlaic required the solitary to proceed to his oratory at the established times for this purpose.[68] Goscelin, according to Dom André Wilmart's summary, assumed that Ève said the office, for he advises her to dedicate all the hours, and especially sext and none, to the suffering of Christ.[69] St. Ailred's sister was to observe the hours *secundum formam regule beati Benedicti*;[70] and the much later Dublin rule specifies the celebration of the hours at their appointed time and further counsels the use of the Penitential Psalms, the Litany of the Saints, and the like.[71] These rules were intended primarily for persons with monastic experience who could therefore be counted on for a full knowledge of the *opus Dei*. With audiences of this sort, the writers of rules were able to dispose rather briefly of the devotional aspect of the solitary life, central though it was.

In decided contrast, the author of *AR*, addressing himself to three young women who had never, so far as we can tell, lived as professed members of a nunnery or passed through a novitiate, felt obliged to devote the whole of one of his "distinctions" — and that the first in his rule — to rather close, elementary directions. Even prior to drawing up his rule, he had evidently been assured that each of his charges had at hand a copy of her own making of the Office of Our Lady, which he specified as the basic element of daily prayer. Beyond this, he felt the need to spell out in Part I the appropriate gestures and postures of worship as well as the many supplementary services to be performed daily. Scattered throughout his discourse are allusions in the form of one-line or even one-word incipits of many prayers, hymns, antiphons, and other formulas. These allusions and also the bare references by title to supplementary observances, such as the offices of the Dead and of the Holy Ghost, could have been intelligible to the anchoress only if, in addition to her copy of the Office of Our Lady, and, of course, of *AR* itself, she had access to other texts, which a book of hours could have provided.[72] Is it possible that she was expected to have copied the whole of such a work rather than the text of the Lady Office alone?

To attempt the identification of a particular medieval "hours" as one close to the anchoress's exemplar, or to elaborate in technical detail on the liturgical tradition drawn upon by the devotions in *AR*, must be considered to lie beyond the scope of the present essay.[73] Nevertheless, one may say that the meager evidence provided by the liturgical cues in Part I suggests that the anchoress's Office of Our Lady did not differ radically from that preserved in two eleventh-century manuscripts edited by E. S. Dewick. Dewick believes that both his texts, which show general agreement with each other, were written for Benedictine nunneries, even though certain of the prescribed psalms reflect an influence other than Benedictine.[74]

The stipulation that the anchoress was to recite not the monastic office, the normal obligation of the earlier recluses, but the Office of Our Lady calls for brief comment. First known in the tenth century, this office, or "little office," as it was often called, was modeled on the Divine Office. That is, a service was provided for all the traditional hours, although matins contained no more than a single nocturn of three psalms and three lessons in place of the three nocturns of the Benedictine practice in winter. Also, the psalms of the other hours were invariable instead of changing with the day of the week. Some or all of the Hours of Our Lady are known to have been recited after the corresponding monastic hours in many religious houses, and its continuing popularity is attested by the fact that it became the nucleus of the books of hours.[75] Even before the thirteenth century, it was authorized for use by some communities of women.[76]

Part I of *AR* provides first of all a lengthy set of devotional preparations that was to occupy the anchoress from the moment of awakening until she began her matins. The sign of the cross, the invocation to the Trinity, a hymn with its versicle and response, the meditation on the crucifix with prayers to the five wounds, and the veneration of relics either corresponded exactly to or were compatible with monastic practice at the beginning of the day, as indicated in notes to the text. The *Pater Noster* and Creed which the anchoress was to say as the immediate preface to matins were also recited by monks before each of the altars in their church before they entered their stalls in the early morning. Again, in emulation of monastic use, followed as well by seculars, these devotions were to be made in a kneeling position on weekdays and standing with bowed head on Sundays and festivals. In accordance with the pattern established by the Divine Office, the versicle "O Lord, open my lips" began the anchoress's matins, and the succeeding versicle "O Lord, come to my aid" began the other hours except for compline.

The anchoress was next directed to recite the full round of the Lady Office, each hour by itself and at its proper time. That is, the Office of Our Lady seems to have been the main staple of her daily prayer rather than an addendum to the monastic or canonical hours. She was to observe the standard monastic division of the liturgical year—that is, summer was defined for her as the period from Easter to the Feast of the Exaltation of the Cross, 14 September, and winter from 14 September to Easter. Whereas two meals daily were authorized in summer and on Sundays throughout the year, only one was to be eaten in winter, again monastic custom.[77]

The performance of each of the Hours of Our Lady was to be supplemented by the recitation of a number of other devotions, all of them taken from the expanded monastic choir service. These supplements range from short series of prayers or psalms, with associated formulas, to a "little office." Parenthetically, it should be noted that the author expected the anchoress to listen to the canonical hours, some of which he evidently assumed would be recited by a priest in the church to which her anchorage was attached. She was not to recite or sing along with the priest loudly enough to be heard by him. Likewise, she was to observe the daily celebration of Mass at the high altar standing or kneeling by the "squint" in her cell and reciting quietly certain devotions during the elevation of the Host.[78] At the kiss of peace, she is told in a striking passage to allow her soul to pass out of her body in meditation on God's love. At midday, presumably after Mass, she was to venerate the cross, uttering a number of prayers, including five eloquent prayers to the Virgin in English.[79]

For the rest, Part I provides prayers for special intentions, a few of them in English. For example, an extended English form of the *Pater Noster* is given for optional use. Part I closes with miscellaneous instructions and observations, some of them amounting to concessions to an anchoress who might be ill or who might lack the education necessary to read her office. This last provision is surprising in view of the impression we gain of the three original anchoresses, who were not only able to copy out the Office of Our Lady but were also, it seems, capable of reading English, French, and probably some Latin.

Even after making allowance for optional acts of worship, one must conclude that the anchoress's liturgical day was a crowded one. She could scarcely have begun her matins much later than 4:00 in the morning if she heeded her rule, which implies that her daily routine did not differ greatly from that followed by monks and colleges of secular clergy, such as the canons. An attempt to map out the anchoress's *horarium* as prescribed in *AR* is given below. On the basis of such texts of the medieval Office of Our Lady and of other devotions as are available, we can estimate that the anchoress spent not fewer than four hours daily in set prayers and acts of worship. In addition, she attended Mass, taking communion fifteen times annually, listened to the priest's recitation of one or more of the canonical hours, engaged in much private prayer and meditation, and read her rule, the Psalter, and other improving works. Little enough time was left over for instruction of her maidservant, needlework on church vestments, conferences with her spiritual director, and occasional confession.

The primacy of the *opus Dei* in religious life provides a basis for regarding every rule governing that life as first and foremost a prayerbook. This would be true even of rules offering relatively few devotional directives, whose authors could assume that their readers had had prior instruction in such matters. The author of *AR*, as has been suggested, could not make that assumption. Having written his rather full treatise on worship, he may have decided to give it first place in his book principally in order to impress on his anchoresses the fundamental obligation of the life they had chosen. This view prompts some reflections on the author's statement in his Introduction that both the first and last parts of *AR* belong to the outer rule. In the sense that Part I concerns overt acts of worship the statement is true. Yet the anchoress's devotions and her participation in the sacraments were surely understood to possess a transcendent value, a value sometimes expressed in the phrase *ex opere operato*.[80] In short, it was through her immersion in the liturgy, best sustained, to be sure, by governing her inner and outer life in obedience to her rule, that the anchoress might hope for the grace necessary for sanctification. The rule itself, then, both in its inner and outer aspects, could well be considered ancillary to the anchoress's primary obligation of worship and her ultimate spiritual goal.

### The Anchoress's Horarium[81]

| | |
|---|---|
| 3–5 A.M. | Preliminary devotions and prayers |
| | Matins and Lauds of Our Lady (recited *seriatim*) |
| | Dirige (Matins and Lauds of the Office of the Dead) |
| | Suffrages and Commendations |
| | Litany of the Saints (daily except Sundays) |
| | Lauds of the Holy Ghost (optional) |
| 5–6 | Listen to the priest's celebration of the canonical hours when possible |
| 6–7 | Prime of the Holy Ghost (optional) |
| | Prime of Our Lady |
| 7–8 | Preciosa |
| 8–9 | Terce of the Holy Ghost (optional) |
| | Terce of Our Lady |
| 9–10 | Prayers and supplications |
| | Devotions before the cross |
| 10–11 | Devotions to Our Lady |
| | The Seven Penitential Psalms |
| | The Fifteen Gradual Psalms |
| 11–12 | Mass (communion fifteen times annually) |
| 12–1 P.M. | Sext of the Holy Ghost (optional) |
| | Sext of Our Lady |
| | Meal (first meal in summer; only meal on weekdays in winter) |

| 1–2 | None of the Holy Ghost (optional) |
| | None of Our Lady |
| 2–3 | Rest period |
| 3–5 | Private prayers and meditation |
| | Reading in the Psalter, *AR*, and other edifying books in English and French |
| | Instruction of maidservants |
| | Work: plain needlework on church vestments or clothing for the poor |
| | Vespers of the Holy Ghost (optional) |
| | Vespers of Our Lady |
| | Placebo (Vespers of the Office of the Dead, omitted before a feast of nine lessons) |
| | Meal (second meal on Sundays; on weekdays in summer only) |
| 5–7 | Compline of the Holy Ghost (optional) |
| | Compline of Our Lady |
| | Bedtime prayers and devotions |

# Note to the Reader

## *The Text*

The present edition furnishes with few exceptions Scribe A's text as corrected and revised by Scribe B (see General Introduction, p. 5). The few editorial emendations (as distinct from B's revisions) are indicated in the textual notes. Where B occasionally glossed A, that is, wrote a synonym for A's reading without marking the synonym for addition or A's text for deletion, A's text is retained and the gloss relegated to the textual notes.

The many glosses, additions, and deletions by Scribe D, whose grasp of the text was imperfect, have been as far as possible excluded, as have the minor additions and revisions in still other hands. In the difficult matter of distinguishing between B's and D's erasures, we follow E. J. Dobson (Early English Text Society, 267).

MS folio numbers are given within the text between vertical bars. MS lineation has not been preserved. Line numbers in the right margin refer to the edited text only. Capitalization, paragraphing, punctuation, and word division are editorial. In scattered cases editorial word division has resulted in initial *ð*, a violation of scribal orthographic practice (e.g., MS *alðe* "all the" appears in the edited text as *al ðe*). We believe that the sacrifice of orthographic consistency is justified by a gain in readability.

MS *etc.* is left unexpanded. Other MS abbreviations are expanded silently as follows:

7. In Middle English passages MS *7* "and" is expanded to *ant*, the only form in which this coordinating conjunction appears when spelled out by A (Dobson, e.g., fols. 37r5;

88r16, 20) or B (Dobson, e.g., 12r11, note f). In Latin
passages the symbol is expanded to *et*.

ꝥ. MS þ "that" is expanded to *þet* in accordance with the treat-
ment of OE *æ* in the MS. Cf. also *þet* in the hands of A
(e.g., Dobson, 154r2) and B (Dobson, e.g., 4r20, note i).

℣. In medieval Latin works this abbreviation stands for *versiculus* "versicle" and is so expanded here, although the
scribe may have intended synonymous Middle English
*verset*, which alternates with the abbreviated form in the
text.

The following special features of the text should be noted:

*Angle Brackets*. These enclose B's additions and substitutions;
e.g., ⟨mid⟩.

*Square Brackets*. These enclose Dobson's reconstructions of il-
legible text; e.g., [þet].

*Italics*. All Latin passages, except for brief directions pertaining to the conduct of worship, are set in italics.

*Diacritics*. No attempt is made to reproduce MS diacritics. A
diacritic is inserted editorially over the vowel of the second person singular *þé* to distinguish it from the relative
pronoun and the definite article.

## The Translation

In the facing-page translation, italicized passages correspond to
the italicized Latin of the medieval text. Where the Latin in the
medieval text amounts to no more than a fragmentary cue or in-
cipit, the translation includes only as much more of the Latin source
as is necessary to make the syntax of the cue apparent in English.
The superscript numbers in the translation refer to the explanatory
notes.

# Ancrene Riwle

## Introduction

*and*

## Part One

# Ancrene Riwle

## Introduction

|fol. 4ʳ| *"Recti diligunt te." In canticis sponsa ad sponsum.* ⟨E⟩st ⟨r⟩ectum *grammaticum, rectum geometricum, rectum theologicum, et sunt differencie totidem regularum. De recto theologico sermo nobis est, cuius due sunt regule. Vna circa cordis direccionem; altera uersatur circa exteriorum rectificacionem. "Recti diligunt te."*

"Lauerd," seið Godes spuse to hire deorewurðe spus, "þeo richte luuieð þé." Þeo beoð richte þe liuieð efter riwle, ⟨ant ȝe⟩, mine leoue sustren, habbeð moni dei icraued me efter riwle. Moni 10 cunne riwlen beoð, ach twa beoð bimong alle þet ich wille speoken of þurch ower bone ant ⟨mid⟩ Godes grace. Þet an riwleð þe heorte ant makeð efne ant smeðe wiðvte cnoste ant dolke of ⟨woh inwit ant of wreȝinde þet segge⟩, "Her ⟨þu⟩ sunegest," oðer, "Þis nis naut ibet ȝet alse ⟨wel as⟩ hit schulde." Þeos riwle is eauer inwið ant richteð þe heorte. ⟨Ȝef þe concience, þet is, þe inwit of þi þoht ant of þin heorte, bereð witnesse i þe seolf teȝeines þe seoluen þet tu art i sunne unscriuen ant þet tu misdest þet ant þet ant hauest þet unþeaw ant þet, þulli conscience, þullic inwit is woh ant unefne ant cnosti ant dolki. Ah þeos riwle efneð hire 20 ant makeð hire smeðe ant softe⟩. Þeo oðer ⟨riwle⟩ is al wiðvten ant riwleð þe licome ant þe licomliche deden. Heo teacheð al hu me schal beoren him wið⟨uten⟩: hu eoten ant drinken, werien ant singen, slepen ant wak⟨i⟩en. |fol. 4ᵛ| Ant þeos riwle nis naut buten to seruin þa oðer. Þeo oðer is als a lauedi, þeos is alse þuften; for al þet me deð of ordre wiðuten nis buten to riuwlin ðe heorte wiðinnen.

Nu aske ȝe wat riwlen ȝe ancren schulen habben. Ȝe schulen alles weis wið alle michte ant strengðe wel witen þinre, ant þuttere for hire sake. Þinre is eauer ilich; þe vtterre is mislich. For uh 30

# Ancrene Riwle

## Introduction

*"Those who are right love you." In the Canticles,*[1] *the bride speaks thus to the bridegroom. One may speak of rightness in grammar, rightness in geometry, and rightness in theology, and for each of these there are special rules. Our work deals with theological rightness, which has two rules. The first has to do with rightness of heart, the second with righting of external things. "Those who are right love you."*

"Lord," says God's bride to her beloved bridegroom, "those who are right love you." Those who live according to a rule are right, and you, my dear sisters, have on many an occasion begged me to give you a rule. There are many kinds of rules, but, in answer to your request and with God's grace, I will speak of two among all of them. The first rules the heart and makes it even and smooth without lump and pit of crooked and accusing conscience that says, "Here you sin," or, "This is not yet amended as well as it should be." This rule is always within and makes the heart right. If your conscience, that is, the inward moral sense of your thought and your heart, bears witness within yourself against yourself that you are unconfessed in sin and that you do wrong in one thing and another and have this vice and that, such conscience, such inward moral sense is crooked and uneven and lumpy and pitted. But this rule makes her even and smooth and soft. The second rule is altogether external and controls the body and fleshly acts. She teaches fully how one ought to conduct oneself outwardly: how to eat and drink, dress and sing, sleep and keep vigil. And the purpose of this rule is solely to serve the first. The first is like a lady, the second is like a maidservant; for whatever one does in a proper way outwardly is only for the sake of governing the heart within.

Now, you ask what rules you anchoresses should have. You shall always with all might and strength keep well the inner, and for her sake the outer. The inner is ever the same; the outer is var-

an schal halde þuttere efter þet heo best mei wið hire seruin þeo inre.

Nu schal hit swa beon þet alle ancren maʒen halden an riwle wel *quantum ad puritatem cordis circa quam uersatur omnis religio.* Þet is, alle maʒen ant ahʒen halden an riwle anonden purte of heorte, þet is, clene ant schir ⟨inwit, þet is, conscience, þe ne beo weote ne witnesse of nan gret sunne inwið hireseoluen⟩ þet ne beo þurhc schrift ibet. Þis maket þe lauedi riwle, þe riwlet ant smeðeð ant richteð þe heorte ant ⟨þe inwit aʒein⟩ sunne; for naut ne makeð hire ⟨woh, scraggi, ant unefne⟩ bute sunne ane. 10 Richten hire ant smeðen hire is of vh ordre ant of uh religion þe god ant þe strengðe. Þeos riwle nis naut |fol.5ʳ| imaked of monnes findles, ach is of Godes heste. Forþi, heo is eauer an wiðvten changinge, ant alle aʒen hire in an eauer to halden.

Ach alle ne maʒen naut halden ane riwle, ne ne þurue naut, ne ne ahʒe naut halden on ane wise þe vtterre riwle, *quantum scilicet ad obseruancias corporales,* þet is, anonde licomes locunges-efter — þeo vttere riwle, þet ich þuften cleopede ant is monnes findles, for nan þing elles ⟨istalt⟩ bute to seruin þe inre. Þe⟨os uttere riwle þet is i þe ende of þis boc þe eahtuhe distincciun, 20 þet is, þe leaste dale⟩, makeð festen, wakien, calde ant harde werien, ant swich oðere hardschipes þet moni flesch mei þolien ant moni ne mei naut. Forþi, mot þeos riwle changin hire misliche, efter vch anes manere ant efter hire euene, ⟨as hire meistre seið hire, for he bereð þeos riwle inwið his breoste, ant he, efter þet sum is oðer sec oðer hal, scal efter his wit changi þeos uttere riwle efter euch anes euene⟩. For sum is strong, sum vnstrong ant mei ful wel beon quite ant paien God mid lesse. Sum is clergesse ant sum nan ant mot þe mare wurchen ant on oðe⟨r⟩ wise segen hire bonen. Sum is ald ant feble ant is þe lesse 30 dred of; sum is ʒeung ant strong ant |fol.5ᵛ| is neod þe betere warde. Forþi, schal vh ancre habben þe vttere riwle efter hire schriftes red ant hwet se he bit ant hat hire in obedience, þe cnaweð hire manere ant wat hire strengðe. He mai þe vttere riwle changin efter wisdom ase he sið hu þe inre maʒe beon best ihalden.

Nan ancre ne schal bi mi read makien professiun, þet is, bihaten heste alswa ase heste, buten þreo þinges. Þet beoð obedience, chastete, ant studeuest⟨nesse⟩: þet heo ne schal þene stude

iable. For each one shall maintain the outer according to how she may best serve the inner with her.

Now, it must be that all anchoresses shall indeed hold to one rule *regarding the purity of the heart with which all religion is concerned.* That is, all can and ought to hold one rule regarding purity of the heart, that is, a clean and clear inward moral sense, that is, conscience, which neither knows nor is witness of any great sin within herself that is not atoned for through confession. This comprises the "lady" rule, which governs and smoothes and rights the heart and the conscience against sin; for nothing makes the conscience crooked, jagged, and uneven except sin alone. To correct and smooth her is the virtue and strength of every order and every rule. This rule is not of man's invention but is of God's commandment. Therefore, she is always one without change, and all ought to hold to her in the same way forever.

But all persons cannot abide by one rule, nor need nor ought to keep in one way the outer rule, *regarding corporeal observances*, that is, regarding bodily observances—the outer rule, which I called the servant and which is man's invention, established for nothing other than to serve the inner. This outer rule, that is at the end of this book the eighth and final section, ordains fasting, holding vigil, wearing clothes cold and harsh, and such other austerities that the flesh of many can endure and that of many others cannot. Therefore, this rule may change variously, according to each anchoress's condition and ability, as her master tells her, for he bears this rule within his breast; and accordingly as anyone is either sick or well, he will change this outer rule as he judges necessary to suit each one's ability. For one is strong, another weak and can very well be released and satisfy God with less. One is educated and another not and must labor the more and say her prayers differently. One is old and feeble and is the less to be feared for; another is young and strong and has need of closer watch. Therefore, each anchoress shall maintain the outer rule in keeping with her confessor's advice and do obediently whatever he asks and enjoins upon her, for he knows her condition and strength. He may alter the outer rule according to his judgment, as he sees how the inner may best be held.

In my opinion no anchoress ought to make profession, that is, make a vow, also promise in the manner of a vow, except in three things. These are obedience, chastity, and stability of abode: that

neauer mare changin bu⟨te⟩ for nede ane, ase strengðe ant ⟨as
of fur oðer of oþer peril⟩ deaðes drednesse, obedience of hire
bischp oðer of his herre. ⟨ʒe ne schulen, ic segge, makie na ma
uuz of feste biheastes⟩. For hwase nimeð þing on hond⟨e⟩ ant
hit bihat God ase heste to donne, ha bint hire þerto ant sunegeð
deaðliche i þe bruche ʒef heo hit breke⟨ð⟩ willes. Ʒef heo hit ne
bihat naut, heo hit þach mei don ant leaue ⟨h⟩wenne heo wel
wule, ase of mete ant of drunh, flesc forgan oðer fisch, ant alle
oðere swiche þinges, of werunge, of liggunge, of hures, of oðere
beoden seggen. Þeos ant þullich oðere beoð alle i freo wil to don     10
|fol.6ʳ|oðer to leten, hwile me wule ⟨ant hwen me wule⟩, buten
heo beon ⟨bi⟩hoten.

Ach cherite, þet is luue, ant edmodnesse, ant þolemodnesse,
treowschipe ant haldunge of ⟨alle þe⟩ ten hestes, schrift ant
penitence: þeos ant þullich oðere, þeo beoð summe of the alde
laʒe, summe of þe neowe, ne beoð naut monnes findles ach beoð
Godes hestes, ant forþi mot vh mon neodeliche ham holden, ant
ʒe over alle. For þeos riwlið ⟨þ⟩e heorte. Of hire riulunge is al
mest þet ich write, bute i þe frumðe in þis boc ant i þe leste ende.
Þe þinges þet ich write þer of þe vttere riwle, ʒe ham holdeð alle,     20
mine leoue sustren, Vre Lauerd beo hit þonked, ant schule þorch
his grace se lengere se betere. Ant þach, nulle ich naut þet ʒe
bihoten heom ase heste to holden, for ase ofte ase ʒe ⟨þrefter⟩
breke⟨n eni of ham⟩, hit ⟨walde⟩ to swiðe ⟨hurten⟩ ower heorte
ant make⟨n⟩ ou swa offered þet ʒe ⟨muhten⟩ sone, as God
forbeode, fallen ⟨i desesperance, þet is, inte⟩ an vnhope ant ⟨inte⟩
an vnbileaue for to beon iboreʒen. Forþi, þet ich |fol.6ᵛ| write
ou, mine leoue sustren, of uttere þinges in þe eareste dale of ouwer
boc of ouwer seruise, ant nomeliche in þe leste, ʒe ne schule naut
bihaten hit, ach habben hit on heorte ant don hit as ʒe hit hefde     30
bihaten.

Gef ani vnweote askið ou of wat ordre ʒe beoð, ase summe
doð, ʒe telleð me, þe siʒeð þe gnete ant swoleʒeð þe fleʒe, ondswereð, "Of Seint Iames," þe wes Godes apostel ant, for his
muchel halinesse, icleoped Godes broðer. Ʒef him þunche[ð]
wunder ant sullich of swich ondswere, askið hwat beo ordre, ant
hwer he finde in Hali Writ openlukest ⟨religiun⟩ descriuet ant
isutelet. [Þet] is i Seint Iames Pistel. He seið hwat is religiun
ant ⟨h⟩wich is richt ordre. *Religio munda et inmaculata apud Deum,
etc.* Þet is, clene religiun ant wiðvte wem ⟨i⟩s iseon ant helpen     40

is, she shall never again move her dwelling except out of necessity alone, such as when compelled by force, and by fear of death (as, for example, by fire or other peril), or obedience to her bishop or his superiors. You ought not, I say, make any other use of firm vows. For whoever undertakes an obligation and promises God to carry it out as a vow, she binds herself to it and sins mortally in the breaking of it if she breaks it willingly. If she does not vow it, she can nevertheless do it and leave off whenever she wishes, as, for example, concerning food and drink, forgoing flesh or fish, and all other similar matters having to do with apparel, lying abed, or saying of Hours or other prayers. These and such others one is free to do or not, while one wishes and when one wishes, unless they are vowed.

But charity, which is love, and humility, and fortitude, faith and the keeping of all the Ten Commandments, confession and penitence: these and such others, of which some are of the old law, some of the new, are not man's inventions but are God's commandments, and therefore everyone must necessarily keep them, and you above all. For these rule the heart. Most that I write concerns the ruling of her, except in the first and last parts of this book. The things that I write there about the outer rule, you keep them all, my dear sisters, may our Lord be thanked, and you shall through his grace keep them better the longer you keep them. Nevertheless, I do not wish that you promise to keep them as vows, for as often as you should break any of them thereafter, it would pain your heart too much and make you so fearful that you might soon, may God forbid, fall into despair, that is, into a loss of hope and into a loss of faith that you will be saved. Therefore, my dear sisters, what I write you about outward things in the first part and especially in the last part of your book of devotions, you shall not vow it, but hold it in heart and do it as if you had vowed it.

If any ignorant person inquire of what order you are, as you tell me some do, men who strain out the gnat and swallow the fly, reply, "Of the order of St. James," who was God's apostle and, because of his great holiness, called God's brother. If such an answer seems to him remarkable and strange, ask him what is an order, and where in Holy Writ he might find religion most openly explained and made clear. That is in St. James's Epistle. For he says what religion is and what true order is: *Religion pure and spotless before God, etc.* [2] That is, pure religion without spot is to visit and help

widewen ant federlase children ant from þe world witen him clene
ant vnwemmed. Þus Seint Iame descriueð religiun ant ordre.
Þe latere dole of his saȝe limpeð to reclusen, for þer beoð |fol.7ʳ|
twa dalen to twa manere þet beoð of religi⟨use⟩. To eiðer limpeð
his dale, as ȝe maȝen ⟨heren⟩. Gode religiuse beoð summe in
þe world, nomeliche prelaz ant treowe pre[a]ch[i]urs. Þeo habbeð
þe arre dale of þet Seint Iame seide. Þeo beoð, alse he seide, þet
gað to helpe widewen ant federlese children. Þe saule is widewe
þet haueð forloren hire spus, þet is, Iesu Crist, wið ani heaued
sunne. Þeo is alswa federles þet haueð þorch his sunne iloren þene     10
heȝe Feder of heouene. Gan iseon þulliche ant elnin ham ant
helpen mid fode ⟨of⟩ hali lore. Þis is richt religiun, swa he seið
Seint Iame. Þe latere dale of his saȝe limpeð to ouwer religiun,
as ich ear seide, þe witeð ou from þe world ouer oðere religiuse,
clene ant vnwemmed. Þus Seint Iame descriueð religiun. Nouðer
hwit ne blac ne nemmet he in his ordre, ach monie siȝeð þe
gnette ant swoleȝeð þe fleȝe, þet is, makeð muche ⟨strencðe⟩ þer
as is þe leaste.

   Pauwel, þe earest ancre, |fol.7ᵛ| Antonie ant Arsenie,
Macarie, ant ⟨þe oþre hali men sumhwile⟩, neren ha religiuse     20
ant of Seint Iames ordre? Alswa Seinte Sarre ant Seinte
Sinc⟨l⟩ete⟨ce⟩ ant monie oðere swicche, wepmen baðe ant wim-
men, wið hare greate mete[n] ant hare herde hearen, neren heo
of god ordre? Ant hweðer hwite oðer blake, ase vnwise ou askið,
⟨þ⟩e weneð þet ordre sitte in þe curtel, God wat, noðeles, ha were
wel baðe; naut, þach, anonde claðes, ach ase Godes spuse singeð bi hireseoluen, *Nigra sum sed formosa.* "Ich am blac ant þach
hwit," ha seið, vnse[u]liche wiðuten, schene wiðinnen. On þisse
wise ondswereð to þe askeres of oure ⟨ordre: þet ȝe beoð as is
iseit of Sein Iames ordre; ant of þe ilke dale⟩ þet he wrat [þe]     30
la[tere], *Inmaculatum se custodire ab hoc seculo.* Þet is þet ich ou ear
seide: from þe world witen him clene ant vnwemmed. Herin is
religiun, naut i þe wide hod ne i þe blake ne i þe hwite ne in
þe greiȝe cuuel. Þear ase monie beoð igedered togederes, þer for
anrednesse me schal makie strengðe of annesse of claðes ant of
oðer hwet of uttere þinges, þet þe annesse wiðuten bitacni þe
annesse |fol.8ʳ| of an luue ant of an wil þet heo alle habbeð i-
mene wiðinnen. Wið hare abit, þet is an, þet uch an haueð ⟨swuc⟩
as oðer, ant alswa ⟨of⟩ oðer hwet, ha ȝeieð þet heo habbeð alle

widows and fatherless children and keep oneself pure and unspotted from the world. Thus St. James describes religion and order. The latter part of his statement pertains to recluses, for the two parts correspond to the two kinds of religious. To each of the two belongs his own, as you may hear. Some religious in the world are good, especially prelates and true preachers, referred to in the first part of what St. James said. They are those, as he said, who go to help widows and fatherless children. The soul is a widow who has lost her husband, that is, Jesus Christ, because of any mortal sin. That one also is fatherless who, through sin, has lost the high Father of heaven. Go visit such people and comfort and help them with the food of holy teaching. This is true religion, as St. James says. The latter part of his statement pertains to your religion, as I said before, which protects you from the world beyond other religious, pure and unspotted. Thus St. James describes religion. He speaks of neither white nor black in connection with his order, but many strain out the gnat and swallow the fly, that is, make great effort in the least things.

Paul, the first anchorite,[3] Anthony[4] and Arsenius,[5] Macarius,[6] and the other holy men of the past, were they not religious and of St. James's order? Also St. Sarah[7] and St. Sincletia[8] and many other such, both men and women, with their coarse mattresses and hard hair shirts, were they not of a good order? And whether white or black, as the foolish ask you, who believe that order resides in the kirtle, God knows, nevertheless, they were indeed both; not, however, with regard to clothing, but just as God's bride sings by herself, *I am black but fair.*[9] "I am black and yet white," she says, uncomely without, fair within. In this manner reply to those asking about your order: that you are as is said of St. James's order; and, from the same passage, reply what he wrote later, *to keep oneself unspotted from this world.* That is what I said to you before: to keep oneself pure and unspotted from the world. Herein is religion, not in the wide hood nor in the black, white, or gray cowl. Where many are gathered together, there for oneness of thought one ought to stress uniformity of clothing and of other things concerning external matters, so that the uniformity without betokens the uniformity of one love and one will that they all have in common within. By their habit, which is uniform, in which each is just as the others, and also by uniformity of other things, they proclaim that they all

togederes an luue ant an wil, vhc an as oðer. Loke þet heo ne
liȝen.

Þus hit is in couent. Ach hwerse mon ⟨oðer wummon⟩ liueð
bi h⟨a⟩m ane, ermite oðer ancre, of þinges wiðuten, ⟨h⟩warof
⟨scandle⟩ ne c⟨u⟩me, nis naut muche strengðe. Hercne Michee
þe Prophete: *Indicabo te, o homo, quid sit bonum et quid Deus requirat
a te: vtique facere iudicium et iusticiam sollicite ambulare cum Domino
Deo tuo.* "Ich wile schawi þé, mon," seið þe hali Michee, "wat
is god ant hwich religiun ant hwich ordre God askeð of þé. Lo
þis, understond hit: do wel, ant deme ⟨wac euer þeseoluen⟩, ant    10
wið dred ant wið luue gan mid God þi Lauerd." Þer as þeose
þinges beoð, þer is richt religiun, þer is soð ordre; ant al þet oðer
⟨wiðute⟩ þis nis buten a[n] trichunge ant a[n] fals gile. Al þet
gode religiuse doð oðer werieð efter þuttere riwle, al hit is
herefore. Al nis buten tole to timbren her toward. Al nis buten
|fol.8ᵛ| an þuften to seruin þe lauedi to riwlin þe heorte.

Nv, mine leoue sustren, þis boc ic[h] todeale on achte destincciuns, þet ȝe cleopeð dalen, ant vh an wiðvte monglunc spekeð
ase bi himseoluen of sunderliche þinges, ant þach uch an richt
falleð efter þe oðer, ant is þe latere dale iteiȝet to þe arre.        20

Þe eareste dale spekeð al of ower seruise.

Þe oðer is hu ȝe schulen þurch ouwer vif wittes witen ouwer
heorte, þe ordre ant religiun ⟨ant⟩ saule lif is inne. In þis desting-
ciun beoð chapitres fiue, ase vif stuche[n] efter þe vif wittes, þe
witeð þe heorte ase wakemen, hwerse heo beoð treowe, ant spekeð
of vh an [wit] sund[erlepi] areawe.

Þe þridde dale is of fif cunnes fo[w]eles þet Daui in þe Sauter
efneð himseoluen to, as he were ancre, ant hu þe cunde of þilke
fuȝeles ancren beoð iliche.

Þe feorðe dale is of flesliche fondunge ant gastliche baðe, ant   30
cumfort aȝeines ham, ant of hare saluen.

Þe fifte is of schrift.

Þe seste of penitence.

|fol.9ʳ| Þe seoueðe of schir heorte, hwi me schal ant hwi me
ach Iesu Crist luuien, ant hwet binimeð vs his luue ant let vs
him to luuien.

Þe achtuðe dale is al of þe vttere riwle, of þe þinges þe ȝe maȝen
vnderfon ant hwet þinges ȝe maȝe witen oðer habben; þerefter

together have one love and one will, each one as the others. Take
care that they do not lie.

So it is in the convent. But whenever a man or woman lives alone
by himself, a hermit or an anchoress, external considerations matter little, so long as no scandal come about. Hear the Prophet Micah:
*I will show you, O man, what is good and what God requires of you: especially*
*that you judge and do the right and walk anxiously with the Lord your God.* [10]
"I will show you, O man," says the holy Micah, "what is good and
what religion and order God asks of you. Listen to this, understand it: do well, and judge yourself ever to be weak, and walk
with God your Lord in fear and with love." Wherever these things
are, there is right religion, there is true order; and all the rest without
this is only trickery and false deceit. All that good religious do or
wear in accordance with the external rule, all is for this. It is all
only a tool to build toward this end. It is all only a maid to serve
the lady in governing the heart.

Now, my dear sisters, this book I divide into eight distinctions, [11]
that you call parts, and each one speaks without admixture, as if
independent, of separate matters, and yet each one follows prop-
erly after the other, and the subsequent part is linked to the
preceding one.

The first part treats entirely of your service of devotions.

The second is about how you shall, through your five senses,
guard your heart, in which reside order, religion, and the life of
the soul. In this distinction are five chapters, as sections corresponding to the five senses, which guard the heart like watchmen,
wherever they are trustworthy, and they speak of each sense
separately in succession.

The third part is about five kinds of birds that David likened
to himself in his Psalter, [12] as if he were an anchorite, and about
how the nature of these same birds is like that of anchorites.

The fourth part is about fleshly and spiritual temptations both,
and comfort against them, and about their remedies.

The fifth part is about confession.

The sixth part is about penance.

The seventh part is about the clean heart, why one must and
why one ought to love Jesus Christ, and what takes away his love
from us and prevents us from loving him.

The eighth part is altogether about the outer rule, about the things
you may accept and what things you may have in your care or

of ouwer claðes ant of swiche þinges ase þerabuten falleð; þerefter
of ouwer werkes, of doddunge, ant of blodletunge; of ouwer
meidnes riwle, alast, hu ȝe ham schulen leoueliche learen.

own; thereafter, of your clothing and related matters; thereafter, of your work, of hair-cutting, and of blood-letting; finally, of your maidservants' rule, how you ought to teach them lovingly.

# Ancrene Riwle

## Part I

Hwenne ȝe earest ariseð, blesceð ou ant seggeð *In nomine Patris, etc.*, ant biginneð anan *Veni, Creator Spiritus*, wið up[a]heuene echnen ant honden toward heouene, buȝinde a-cneon forðwart o ðe bedde, ant seggeð al þe imne vt mit þe uerset *Emitte spiritum tuum* ant mid þe oreisun *Deus, qui corda fidelium.* Herefter, scheoȝinde ant claðinde ou, seggeð *Pater Noster* ant *Credo in Deum. Iesu Criste, Fili Dei uiui, miserere nostri, qui de uirgine dignatus es* ⟨*nasci, miserere nobis*⟩. Þeose wordes seggeð ⟨a þet⟩ ȝe beon greiðe. Þis word habbeð muchel an vs |fol.9ᵛ| ant in muðe ofte hwenne ȝe maȝen, sitte ⟨ȝe⟩ oðer stonden.

Hwenne ȝe beoð al greiðe, sprenget ou mid hali water þet ȝe schulen eauer habben, ant þencheð on Godes flesch ant on his blod þet is abuue þe heȝe weoued, ant falleð acneon þertoward mit þeose gretunges:

*Aue, principium nostre creacionis.*
*Aue, precium nostre redempcionis.*
*Aue, viaticum nostre peregrinacionis.*
*Aue, premium nostre expectacionis.*

*Tu esto nostrum gaudium,*
*Qui es futurus premium.*
*Sit nostra in te gloria*
*Per cuncta semper secula.*

*Mane nobiscum, Domine.*
*Noctem obscuram remoue.*
*Omne delictum ablue.*
*Piam medelam tribue.*

# Ancrene Riwle

## Part I

Upon first arising, cross yourself[1] and recite *In the name of the Father, etc.*, and commence immediately *Come, Creator Spirit*[2] with eyes and hands upraised to heaven, bending forward on your knees on the bed, and say the entire hymn with the versicle *Send forth your spirit*[3] and the prayer *God, who taught the hearts of the faithful.*[4] Thereafter, while putting on your shoes and dressing, say the *Our Father* and *I believe in God.*[5] Then say *Jesus Christ, son of the living God, have mercy upon us, you who condescended to be born of a virgin, have mercy upon us.*[6] Say these words until you are dressed. Whether you sit or stand, make much use of this prayer and keep it on your tongue when you can.

When you are fully dressed, sprinkle yourself with holy water, which you shall always keep by you, and think about the flesh and blood of God who is above the high altar,[7] and fall on your knees toward him with these greetings:

> *Hail, author of our creation.*
> *Hail, price of our redemption.*
> *Hail, sustenance of our pilgrimage.*
> *Hail, reward of our hope.*[8]

> *Be our joy,*
> *Who will be our reward.*
> *May our glory be in you*
> *Throughout all eternity.*[9]

> *Remain with us, O Lord.*
> *Take away the dark night.*
> *Wash away all sin.*
> *Bestow holy relief.*[10]

*Gloria tibi, Domine,*
*Qui natus ⟨es de uirgine,*
*etc.⟩*

Aswa ȝe schule don hwenne me hald ⟨hit⟩ vp ed þe messe ant
bifore þe *Confiteor* hwen ȝe schule beon ihuslet. Efter þis, falleð
acneon to þe crucifix mid þase vif gretunges in þe munegunge
of þe vif wunden: *Adoramus te, Criste, et benedicimus tibi, quia per*
*sanctam crucem redemisti mundum. Tuam crucem adoramus, Domine.*
*Tuam gloriosam recolimus passionem. Miserere nostri,* |fol.10ʳ|*qui*
*passus es pro nobis.*       10

*Salue, crux sancta,*
*Arbor digna,*
*Cuius robur preciosum*
*Mundi tulit talentum.*

*Salue, crux, que in corpore Cristi dedicata es et ex membris eius tanquam*
*ex margaritis ornata.*

*⟨O⟩ crux, lignum triumpha⟨le⟩*
*Mundi, uera salus, uale.*
*Inter ligna nullum tale*
*Fronde, flore, germine.*      20

*Medicina Cristiana,*
*Salua sanas, egras sana.*

Ant wið þis word beateð on ouwer heorte:

*Quod non ualet vis humana,*
*⟨Sit in⟩ tuo nomine.*

Hwase ne con þeos viue, segge þe eareste, *Adoramus,* cneolinde
vif siððen, ant blescit ou ed uh an; ant wið þeose wordes, *Miserere*
*nostri, qui passus es pro nobis,* beateð ouwer b⟨r⟩eoste ant cusse⟨ð⟩
þe eorðe, icrucc⟨h⟩ed mid þe þume. Þerefter wendeð ou to Vre
Lauedi onlicnes⟨se⟩ ant cneolið, mit fiue *Auees.* Alast to þe oðer  30
imaines ant to þe relikes luteð oðer cneoleð, nomeliche to þe
haleȝen þet ȝe habbeð to þurh luue iturnd ouwer weouedes, swa

> *Glory be to you, O Lord,*
> *Who were born of a virgin,*
> *etc.* [11]

This you shall do when the Host is held up at Mass and before the *I Confess*[12] on days when you take communion. After that, fall on your knees before the crucifix with these five greetings in memory of the five wounds: *We adore you, O Christ, and bless you, because through your holy cross you redeemed the world.* [13] *We adore your cross, O Lord. We meditate on your glorious passion. Have mercy upon us, you who suffered for us.* [14]

> *Hail, holy cross,*
> *Worthy tree,*
> *Whose precious wood*
> *Bore the treasure of the world!*[15]

*Hail, cross, you who were consecrated to the body of Christ and ornamented with his limbs as with pearls.* [16]

> *O cross, wood triumphant*
> *Over the world, true salvation, hail.*
> *Among woods there is none such*
> *With respect to leaf, flower, or bud.*
>
> *Christian medicine,*
> *Save the healthy, heal the sick.*

And with this word beat your breast, saying,

> *Whatever human strength cannot do,*
> *Let it be done in your name.* [17]

Whoever does not know these five, let her recite the first, *We adore*, five times, while kneeling, and cross yourself with each; and saying these words, *Have mercy upon us, you who suffered for us,* [18] beat your breast and kiss the ground, crossed with the thumb. Then turn to Our Lady's image and kneel, with five *Hail Marys*. Finally, bow or kneel to the other images and relics, especially those of the saints to whom out of love you have dedicated your altars, and

muche þe raðere ȝef ani is ihaleȝed.

Þerefter anan Vre Lauedi Vtsong seggeð on þisse wise. Ȝef
hit his werke dai, falleð to þen eorðe. Ȝef hit is hali dai, buȝinde
sumdel duneward, segeð *Pater Noster* ant |fol.10ᵛ| *Credo*, ba stille.
Richteð ou vp þerefter ed *Domine, labia mea* ant markeð on ower
muð an cros mid þe þume. Ant ed *Deus, in adiutorium* makeð an
cros from þe foreheaued to þe breoste; ant falleð to þer eorðe,
ȝef hit is werke dei, wið *Gloria*; oðer buȝeð duneward, ȝef hit
bið hali dai, oðet *sicut erat*. Þus et vh *Gloria Patri*, ant ed þe bigin-
nunge of þe *Venite*, ant ed *Venite, adoremus*, ant ed þe *Aue Maria*,   10
ant hwerse ȝe eauer hereð Marie nome inempnet; ant to vh *Pater
Noster* þet falleð to þe vres, ant to þe Crede, ant to þe collecte
ed eauer vh tide, ant to þe latemeste vers of eauer vh imne, ant
ed þe leste uers buten an of *Benedicite omnia*. Et alle þeos ilke,
ȝef hit is hali dai, buȝeð sumdel donewart; ȝef hit is werke dai,
falleð to þeorðe. Et þe biginning of eauer vh tide, wið *Deus, in
adiutorium* makeð þe rode taken, as ich ear ou tachte. Et *Veni,
Creator* buȝeð oðer cneolið efter þet þe dei is. Wið *Memento, salutis
autor* falleð eauer adun, ant ed þis word, *Nascendo formam sumpseris*, cusset þe eorðe; ant alswa in þe *Te Deum* et þisse worde,   20
*Non oruisti Virginis vterum*; ant ed þe masse in þe muchele Crede
ed *ex Maria* |fol.11ʳ| *Virgine et homo factus est*.

Evch an segge hire vres as ha haueð iwriten ham ant vh tide
sunderliche ase forð as ha mei ant in his time; ear to sone þenne
to lete, ȝef ȝe þe 〈rihte〉 time 〈ne mahen〉 halden. Vtsong in winter
bi nachte, i somer i þe daȝinge. 〈Þis〉 winter schal biginnen ed
þe Halirode Dai in heruest ant leasten oðet Aster. Prime i winter
earliche, i sumer biforð mareȝen; *Preciosa* þerefter. Ȝef ȝe habbeð neode for ani hichðe to speken, ȝe muȝen seggen hit biforen
ant efter vchtsong anan, ȝef swa neodeð. 〈Non〉 efter mete (ant   30
〈h〉wenne ȝe slepeð, efter slep) hwile þet sumer leasteð, bute
hwenne ȝe festeð; i winter bifore mete hwenne ȝe al festeð; þe
Sunnendei efter mel, for ȝe eoteð twien. Ed þet an salm ȝe schule
stonden, ȝef ȝe beoð aise, ant ed 〈þe oþer〉 sitten; ant eauer wið
þe *Gloria* rungen vp ant buȝen. Hwase mei stonden, aa on Vre
Lauedi wurchipe stonde a Godes halue. Ed alle þe seoue tiden
seggeð *Pater Noster* ant *Aue Marie*, ba biforen ant efter; *Fidelium*

in particular any altars that have been consecrated.

Immediately thereafter, recite Our Lady's Matins[19] in this manner. If on a feria, fall to the ground.[20] If a feast day, bowing a little, say *Our Father* and the *I believe*, both silently. Then rise up at *O Lord, open my lips*[21] and sign a cross on your mouth with the thumb. And at *God, come to my aid* make a cross from the forehead to the breast; and fall to the ground, if it is a feria, saying *Glory be to the Father*; or bow down, if it is a feast day, until *as it was in the beginning*. Do this with every *Glory be to the Father*, and at the beginning of *O come, let us praise the Lord*,[22] and at *Come, let us adore*, and at the *Hail Mary*, and whenever you hear Mary's name spoken; and do the same at each *Our Father* occurring in the hours, and at the Creed, and at the collect in each hour, and at the last verse of every hymn, and at the last verse but one of *Bless the Lord, all you works*.[23] On all these occasions, bow down somewhat if it is a feast day; if a feria, fall to the ground. At the opening of every hour, make the sign of the cross at *God, come to my aid*, as I explained to you before. At *Come, Creator Spirit* bow or kneel according to what day it is. At *Be mindful, author of salvation* always fall, and at this passage, *At birth you assumed our form*,[24] kiss the ground; and do the same in *We praise you, O God* at this passage, *You did not abhor the Virgin's womb*;[25] and likewise in the great Creed of the Mass at *and was incarnate of the Virgin Mary by the Holy Ghost and was made man*.[26]

Let each one say her hours as she has copied them out[27] and, as far as she can, each hour by itself and at its proper time; but if you cannot hold to the right time, rather too soon than too late. Say matins at night in the winter, at dawn in the summer. For this purpose winter shall begin on Holy Cross Day[28] in autumn and continue until Easter. In winter say prime early, in summer, before dawn; say *Precious in the sight of the Lord*[29] thereafter. If you have need to speak because of any urgency,[30] you may do so before and immediately after matins, if necessary. Say none after eating (and when you sleep, after sleeping) during summer, except when you are fasting. In the winter say it before your meal when you all fast; but on Sundays, because you eat twice, after the first meal. At the first psalm you must stand, if you can well do so, and sit at the second; and always at *Glory be to the Father* rise and bow. Whoever can stand, in worship of Our Lady let her always stand, for the sake of God. At all the seven hours say the *Our Father* and *Hail Mary*, both at the beginning and at the end; and *The souls of*

*anime* efter vh tide bifore þe *Pater Noster.* Ed þe þreo tiden seggeð
*Pater Noster* wið Crede: biforen vchtsong ant et prime ant et compelin. From ouwer compelin oðet *Preciosa* beo iseid, haldeð
silence.

Efter euensong anan *Placebo* vhche nicht seggeð, ȝef |fol.11ᵛ|
ȝe beoð aise, bute hit beo hali nicht for feste of niȝe leceons þe
comeð ine mareȝen. Bifore compelin oðer efter vchtsong, *Dirige,*
wið þreo salmes ant wið þreo leceons vche nicht sundri. Ant ȝef
hit bið ani munedai of ouwer leoue front, seggeð alle niȝene.
In þe stude of *Gloria Patri* et vche salmes ende segeð *Requi⟨e⟩m*  10
*eternam* ⟨*dona eis, Domine, et lux perpetua luceat eis.* Ed *Pla*⟩*cebo* ⟨*sitteð*⟩
oðet *Magnificat* ant assw⟨a⟩ et *Dirige,* buten et þe leocuns. ⟨Þear
stondeð⟩ ant et þe *Miserere* ant from þe *Laudate* to þen ende. *Re-*
*quiescant in pace* in þe stude of *Benedicamus.* In þe mareȝen oðer
in nicht efter þe suffragies — ⟨þet beoð þe memoires of þe
halhen⟩ — of vchtsong seggeð commendaciun, sittinde þe salmes,
þe oreisuns cneolinde oðer stondinde. Ȝef ȝe þus doð vche nicht
bute Sunnenicht ane, ȝe doð muche þe betere.

Seoue Salmes seggeð, sittinde oðer cneolinde, wið þe letanie.
Fiftene Salmes seggeð on þisse wise: þe eareste fiue for ouseolf  20
ant for alle þet ou god doð oðer god vnnen; þe oðere fiue for
þe peas of Hali Chirche; þe þridde fiue for alle Cristene saule.
Efter þe forme fiue, |fol.12ʳ| *Kirieleyson; Criste eleyson; Kirieleyson;*
*Pater noster . . . et ne nos . . . sed libera. Saluos fac seruos tuos et an-*
*cillas tuas, Deus meus, sperantes in te.* Oremus. *Deus, cui proprium*
*est misereri.* Efter þoðer fiue, alswa *Kirieleyson; . . . et ne nos. Domine,*
*fiat pax in uirtute tua* ⟨*et habundancia in turribus tuis*⟩. Oremus. *Ec-*
*clesie tue quesumus, Domine, preces placatus,* ⟨*etc.*⟩. Efter þe þridde
fiue ȝe schule seggen — wiðvten *Gloria Patri* — *Kirieleyson; Pater*
*Noster . . . et ne nos; A porta* ⟨*inferi erue, Domine, animas eorum*⟩.  30
Oremus. *Fidelium,* ⟨*etc.*⟩. Seoue Salmes ant Fiftene seggeð abuten
vnder; for abuten swic time ase me singeð masse in alle religiuns
⟨ant⟩ vre Lauerd þolede pine vpon þe rode, ȝe aȝen to beon
nomeliche ibeoden ⟨ant ibenen⟩, ant alswa from prime oðet

*the faithful*[31] after each hour and before the *Our Father*. At the following three hours say the *Our Father* with the Creed: before matins and at prime and at compline. From your compline until *Precious in the sight of the Lord* is said, keep silence.

Every night immediately after evensong say *I will be pleasing to the Lord*,[32] if you can well do it, unless it is the holy night preceding a feast of nine lessons[33] that comes on the next day. Before compline or after matins, say *Direct, O Lord*,[34] with three psalms and three lessons each night. And if it should be a day of remembrance for your dear friends, recite all nine. In place of *Glory be to the Father* at the end of each psalm, say *Lord, grant them eternal rest and let perpetual light shine on them*.[35] Sit at *I will be pleasing to the Lord* until *My soul magnifies the Lord*,[36] and sit also during the *Direct, O Lord*, except at the lessons. At the lessons stand and at *Have mercy upon me*[37] and from *O praise God*[38] to the end. Say *May they rest in peace*[39] in place of *Let us bless the Father*.[40] In the morning or at night after the suffrages of matins — which are in commemoration of the saints — say commendations,[41] sitting for the psalms and for the prayers kneeling or standing. If you do this every night except for Sunday, you will do much the better.

Say the Seven Psalms,[42] sitting or kneeling, along with the litany of the saints.[43] Recite the Fifteen Psalms[44] in this fashion: the first five for yourself and for all who do good to you and wish you well; the second five for the peace of Holy Church; the third five for all Christian souls. After the first five say *Lord, have mercy upon us; Christ, have mercy upon us; Lord, have mercy upon us*; then *Our Father . . . and lead us not into temptation but deliver us from evil*. Then say *Save your servants and handmaidens, who put trust in you, my God*.[45] Let us pray. *God, whose property is always to have mercy*.[46] After the second five say also *Lord, have mercy upon us; . . . and lead us not into temptation*. Then *O Lord, may there be peace in your strength and prosperity in your palaces*.[47] Let us pray. *O Lord, we beseech you, receive mercifully the prayers of your Church, etc.*[48] After the third five — omitting *Glory be to the Father* — you must say *Lord, have mercy upon us; Our Father . . . lead us not into temptation*; and then *O Lord, deliver their souls from the gate of hell*.[49] Let us pray. *O God, creator and redeemer of all the faithful, etc.*[50] Recite the Seven Psalms and the Fifteen Psalms at about mid-morning; for at about the time that mass is sung in all religious houses and our Lord suffered torment on the cross, you ought especially to be in prayers and supplications, and also from prime

midmareȝen, ⟨h⟩wenne preostes of þe world singeð heore messen.

On þisse wise ȝe maȝen, ȝef ȝe wulleð, seggen oure *Pater Nosteres*: "Almichtin God, Feder, Sune, Hali Gast, ase ȝe beoð þreo an God, aswa ȝe beoð an michte, an wisdom, ant an luue; ant þach is michte iturnt to þé in Hali Write, nomeliche þu, deorewurðe Fader; to þé wisdom, seli Sune; to þé luue, Hali Gast." ⟨Neomeð þenne þé up⟩. "Ȝef me, ⟨þu an al⟩mihti God, þrile in þreo hades, |fol.12ᵛ| þeos ilke þreo þinges: michte ⟨for te⟩ serui þé, wisdom for to queme þé, luue ant wil to don hit; mihte, þet ich maȝe don, wisdom, þet ich cunne don, luue, þet ich wulle don al þet þé is leouest. Ase þu art ful of euch good, ase nis nan good wane þer as þeos þreo beoð, michte ant wisdom ant luue ⟨ifeȝet⟩ togederes, þet þu ȝetti me ham, Hali Prumnesse, ⟨i þe⟩ wurchipe of þé." Preo *Pater Nosteres*; *Credo in Deum* wið his uerset *Benedicamus Patrem et Filium, laudemus et super exaltemus.* Oremus. *Omnipotens sempiterne Deus, qui dedisti famulis tuis in confessione, ⟨etc.⟩. Alpha et omega.* Hwase hit haueð al oðer sum oðer of þe Hali Prumnesse, segge wase wulle.

"A, Iesu þin are. Iesu, for mine sunnen honge⟨d⟩ o rode, for þilke fif wunden þe þu on hire bleddest, hel mi blodi saule of ⟨al þe blodi sunnen þet ha is wið iwundet þurh⟩ mine fif wittes; in þe mungunge of ham þet hit swa mote beon, deorewurðe Lauerd." Fif *Pater Nosteres* ant versiculus *Omnis terra adoret te, Deus.* Oremus. *Iuste Iudex.*

"For þe seoue ȝeouen of þe Hali Gast, |fol.13ʳ| þet ich ham mote habben, ant for þe seoue tiden þe Hali Chirche singeð, þet ich deale in ham, ⟨slepe ic oðer wakie⟩, ant for þe seoue bonen in þe *Pater Noster* aȝein þe seouen heaued ant dedliche sunnen, þet þu wite me wið ham ant alle heore strunden, ant ȝeue me þe seouene seli eadinessen þet þu hauest, Lauerd, ⟨bihaten⟩ þine icorene in þin eadi nome." Seoue *Pater Nosteres*; versiculus *Emitte spiritum tuum ⟨et creabuntur et renovabis faciem terre⟩.* Oremus. *Deus, cui omne cor patet, ⟨etc.⟩. Ecclesie tue quesumus, ⟨Domine, etc.⟩. Exaudi quesumus, domine, supplicum preces.*

"For þe ten hestes þet ich ibroken habbe, summe oðer alle, ant meseolf toward þé ⟨h⟩watse beo of oðer hwat vntreoweliche ⟨iteoheðet⟩, in bote of þeose bruchen,, for to sachtni wið þé, deorewurðe Lauerd." Ten *Pater Nosteres*; versiculus *Ego dixi,*

to mid-morning, when secular priests sing their masses.

You may, if you choose, say your *Our Fathers* in this way: "Almighty God, Father, Son, Holy Ghost, just as you three are one God, so are you one power, one wisdom, and one love; and yet in Holy Scripture power is ascribed in particular to you, beloved Father; wisdom to you, blessed Son; and love to you, Holy Ghost." Then stand up and say, "Give to me, you one almighty God, threefold in three persons, these same three qualities: strength to serve you, wisdom to please you, and love and desire to do it; strength, that I can do, wisdom, that I know how to do, love, that I want to do all that is dearest to you. As you are full of every good, and as no good is lacking where these three are present, strength, wisdom, and love united together, may you grant them to me, Holy Trinity, in worship of you."[51] Then say three *Our Fathers*; *I believe in God* with its versicle *Let us bless the Father and Son, let us praise and exalt him forever.*[52] *Let us pray. Almighty and everlasting God, who have given to your servants by the confession of true faith, etc.*[53] Then say *Alpha and omega.*[54] Whoever knows all of this or something else pertaining to the Holy Trinity, let say it who wishes.

"Ah, Jesus, I beg for your mercy. Jesus, who for my sins was hung on the cross, for the same five wounds from which you bled on it, heal my bloody soul of all the bloody sins with which she is wounded through my five senses. In the memory of them that it might be so, beloved Lord."[55] Say five *Our Fathers* and the versicle *Let all the earth worship you, O God.*[56] *Let us pray. O righteous Judge.*[57]

"For the seven gifts of the Holy Ghost,[58] that I may possess them, and for the seven hours that Holy Church celebrates,[59] that I may participate in them, whether I sleep or wake, and for the seven petitions in the *Our Father*[60] against the seven capital and deadly sins, that you guard me from them and all their breed,[61] and give me the seven blessed beatitudes[62] which you, O Lord, have promised your chosen ones in your blessed name." Say seven *Our Fathers*; say the versicle *Send forth your spirit and they will be created and you will renew the face of the earth. Let us pray. God, to whom every heart is open, etc.*[63] *We beseech you, O Lord, hear the prayers of your Church, etc. We beseech you, O Lord, hear the prayers of suppliants.*[64]

"For the ten commandments that I have broken, some or all, and for whatever there be of other things that I have unfaithfully tithed with respect to you, as a remedy for these misdoings, in order to become reconciled to you, beloved Lord." Say ten *Our Fathers*;

*Domine, miserere mei.* Oremus. *Deus, cui proprium est.*

"In þe wurchipe, Iesu Crist, of þine tweolf apostles, þet ich mote over al foleȝen hore lare ant þorh hare bone habbe þe tweolf boȝes þe bloweð of cherite, ase Seint Powel seið, blisfule Lauerd." Teweolf *Pater Noster*; versiculus *Annunciaverunt opera Dei, ⟨et facta eius intellexerunt⟩.* Oremus. *Exaudi nos, Deus, salutaris noster; et apostolorum tuorum, ⟨etc.⟩.*

Haleȝen, ase |fol.13ᵛ| ȝe luuieð mest, in heore wurchipe seg-geð ⟨*Pater Nosteres,* oðer⟩ ma oðer lees, as ow ⟨on⟩ heorte bereð, ant þe verset ⟨þer⟩mid wið hare collecte.                                   10

"For alle þeo þe habbeð ani good idon me, iseid, ant ivnnen, ant for alle þeo ilke þe wurcheð þe six werkes of milce, milcefule Lauerd." Six *Pater Noster*; verset *Dispersit, dedit.* Oremus. *Retribuere dignare*; ant hwase wule, segge bifore þe *Pater Noster* þeos salm: *Ad te leuaui*; ant *Kirieleyson.*

"For hare alre saule þe beoð forð faren i þe bileaue of þe fouwer godspelles þet haldeð al Cristendom vpon fouwer halues, þet þu þe fouwer mar⟨h⟩eȝeuen ȝeue ham in heouene, milcefule Lauerd." Fouwer *Pater Noster*; ⟨ant ȝef ȝe seggeð nihene (as þer beoð nihene englene weoredes) þet God þurh his merci hihe ham   20 ut of pine to hare feorredne, ȝe doð ȝette betere. Ant her aswa, ȝef ȝe wulleð, seggeð⟩ *De profundis* bifore þe *Pater Noster*; versiculus *A porta inferi.* Oremus. *Fidelium.*

Bi deie ⟨sum time⟩ oðer bi nihcte, ⟨gederið in ower heorte alle seke ant⟩ sarie, þe ⟨wa þet poure þolieð, þe pinen⟩ þet prisuns ⟨þolieð⟩ þer heo ligeð wið iren ibunden heuie, nomeliche of þe Cristene þet beoð in heaðenesse, summe in prisun, summe in ⟨ase⟩ muchele þouwedomes as oxnen oðer assen, ant of þeo þet habbeð stronge fondunge⟨s⟩. Alle |fol.14ʳ| menne sares setteð in oure heorte ant sikeð to Vre Lauerd þet ⟨him neome⟩ reuðe  30 of ham ant bihalde toward ham wið þe echȝe of his are. Ant ȝef ȝe habbeð hwile, seggeð *Leuaui oculos* ⟨*meos in montes* ant swa al þe salm ut⟩. *Pater noster . . . et ne nos*; versiculus *Conuertere, Domine. Usquequo? Et deprecabilis esto super seruos tuos.* Oremus. *Pretende, Domine, famulis, ⟨etc.⟩.*

In þe Masse, ⟨h⟩wenne þe preost heueð vp Godes licome, seg-

say the versicle *I have said, O Lord, have mercy upon me.*[65] Let us pray. *God, whose property is always to have mercy.*

"In honor, O Jesus Christ, of your twelve apostles, that I may in all ways follow their teaching and through their prayers have the twelve branches that bloom from love, as St. Paul says,[66] O blessed Lord." Say twelve *Our Fathers*; say the versicle *They declared the works of God, and they understood his deeds.*[67] Let us pray. *Hear us, God, our salvation; and watch over us with the defenses of your apostles, etc.*[68]

In honor of the saints whom you most love, say *Our Fathers*, either more or fewer, as your own heart dictates, and the versicle therewith along with their collect.

"For all who have done to me, said to me, or wished for me any good, and for all the same ones who have performed the six works of mercy,[69] O merciful Lord." Say six *Our Fathers*; say the versicle *He has disposed, he has given.*[70] Let us pray. Say *Deign to reward;*[71] and let whoever wishes say this psalm before the *Our Father*: *To you I have lifted up;* and *Lord have mercy upon us.*

"For the souls of all those who have died in the belief of the four gospels that sustain all Christendom on four sides, that you give them the four marriage portions[72] in heaven, merciful Lord." Say four *Our Fathers*; and if you say nine (since there are nine orders of angels)[73] to the end that God in his mercy may bring souls out of torment into their fellowship, you will do still better. And here also, if you wish, say *Out of the deep*[74] before the *Our Father*; say the versicle *O Lord, deliver their souls from the gates of hell.* Let us pray. *O God, creator and redeemer of all the faithful.*[75]

At some time during the day or night, gather in your heart all the sick and sorrowful, the woe that the poor suffer, the torments that prisoners endure there where they lie heavily bound in irons, especially the torments of the Christians who are in heathendom, some in prison, some in as much servitude as oxen or asses, and of those who experience strong temptations. Implant all men's sorrows in your heart and sigh to Our Lord that he take pity on them and that he look upon them with the eye of his grace. And if you have time, say *I have lifted up my eyes to the mountains*[76] and so the whole psalm to the end. Say *Our Father . . . and lead us not into temptation*; say the versicle *Return, O Lord. How long? And be open to entreaty by your servants.*[77] Let us pray. *Stretch forth, O Lord, to your servants, etc.*[78]

In the Mass, when the priest elevates God's body, recite this verse

geð þis uers stondinde: *Ecce, salus mundi, uerbum Patris, hostia uera, viua caro, deitas integra, uerus homo.* Ant þenne falleð adun mid þeose gretunge:

> *Aue, principium nostre creacionis.*
> *Aue, precium nostre redempcionis.*
> *Aue, viaticum nostre peregrinacionis.*
> *Aue, premium nostre expectacionis.*

> *Tu esto nostrum gaudium,*
> ⟨*Qui es futurus premium.*
> *Sit nostra in te gloria*        10
> *Per cuncta semper secula*⟩.

> *Mane nobiscum,* ⟨*etc.*⟩

> *Gloria tibi, Domine,*
> ⟨*etc.*⟩

*Sed quis est locus in me quo ueniat, in me Dominus quo ueniat et maneat in me, Deus, qui fecit celum et terram? Itane, Domine, Deus meus, est quicquam in me quod capiat te? Quis michi dabit ut uenias in cor meum et inebries illud et vnum bonum meum amplectar te? Quid michi es? Miserere ut loquar. Angusta est tibi domus anime mee. Quo uenias ad eam, dilatetur abs te. Ruinosa est; refice eam. Habet que offendant oculos tuos* |fol.14ᵛ| 20 *fateor et scio, sed quis mundabit eam? Aut cui alteri preter te clamabo? Ab ocultis meis munda me, Domine, et ab alienis parce famule tue.*

*Miserere, miserere, miserere mei, Deus,* ant al ðe salm wið *Gloria. Criste, audi nos. Kirieleyson. Pater Noster. Credo . . . carnis. Saluam fac famulam tuam, Deus meus, sperantem in te. Domine, exaudi . . . et clamor meus.*

Oremus. *Concede, quesumus, omnipotens Deus, ut quem enigmatice et sub aliena specie cernimus, quo sacramentaliter cibamur in terris, facie ad faciem eum uideamus, eo sicuti est ueraciter et realiter frui mereamur* 30 *in celis per eundem Dominum.*

Efter þe Messe-cos, hwen þe preost sacreð, þer forȝeoteð al þe world. Þer beoð al vt of bodie. Þer in sperclinde luue biclup-

standing: *Behold the savior of the world, the word of the Father, true sacrifice, living flesh, entire godhead, very man.*[79] And then fall with this greeting:

> *Hail, author of our creation.*
> *Hail, price of our redemption.*
> *Hail, sustenance of our pilgrimage.*
> *Hail, reward of our hope.*

> *Be our joy,*
> *Who will be our reward.*
> *May our glory be in you*
> *Throughout all eternity.*

> *Remain with us, etc.*

> *Glory be to you, O Lord,*
> *etc.*[80]

*But what place is there in me where he may come, in which the Lord God who made heaven and earth may come and remain in me? Is it so, O Lord my God, is there anything in me which can contain you? Who will grant to me that you may come into my heart and inebriate it and that I may embrace you, my one good? What are you to me? Have mercy that I may speak. The house of my soul is too narrow for you. So that you may enter it, let it be enlarged by you. It is ruinous; repair it. I confess and know it has those things in it which offend your eyes, but who will clean it? But to whom else shall I cry out except to you? From my secret sins cleanse me, O Lord, and from other faults spare your servant.*[81]

Say *Have mercy, have mercy, have mercy on me, God,*[82] and say the remainder of the psalm with *Glory be to the Father. O Christ, hear us. Lord have mercy upon us. Our Father. I believe . . . of the flesh. Save your servant, my God, trusting in you. O Lord, hear my prayer . . . and let my cry come to you.*

Let us pray. *Grant, we beseech you, almighty God, that him whom we see darkly and under a different form, on whom we feed sacramentally on earth, we may see face to face, and that we may be worthy to enjoy him in heaven just as he truly and really is, through the same Lord.*[83]

After the Mass-kiss,[84] when the priest consecrates the elements, there forget all the world. There be entirely out of the body. There in shining love embrace your beloved who has alighted into your

peð ouwer leofmon þet into ouwer breosten bur is ilicht of heouene, ant haldeð him hetefeste oðet he habbe iȝetted ou al þet ȝe wulleð.

Abute middei hwase mei, oðer sumtime, þenche on Godes rode ase heo mest mei ant of his deorewurðe pine, ant biginne þerefter þilke fif gretunges þe beoð iwrite þruppe, ant alswa cneoli to vh an, |fol.15ʳ| ant blesci as hit seið þear, ant beate þe breoste, ant make a þulli bone: *Adoramus te, Criste. Tuam crucem. Salue, crux sancta. Salue, crux que. O crux, lignum.*

Ant arise þenne, ant biginne þe ante⟨f⟩ne *Salua nos, Criste*, ant 10 segge stondinde þe salm *Iubilate* wið *Gloria*, ant þenne seggeð þe ante⟨f⟩ne vt þus: *Salua ⟨nos⟩, Criste saluator, per uirtutem sancte crucis,* ant blesci hire; þenne *Qui saluasti Petrum in mari, miserere nobis,* ant beateð þe breoste, ant þenne fal⟨leð⟩ adun ant seggeð *Criste, audi nos. ⟨Criste, audi nos⟩. Kirieleyson; ⟨Criste eleyson; Kyrieleyson⟩. Pater noster . . . et ne nos. Protector noster, aspice, Deus, et respice in faciem Cristi tui.* Oremus. *Deus, qui sanctam crucem.*

Eft bigin *Adoramus* as ear, alle fiue; *Salua nos, Criste* þe ante⟨f⟩ne as ear; þe salm *Ad te leuaui*; þenne þe antefne al vt; ant þenne falle to þe eorðe as ear. *Criste, audi nos. Kirieleyson. Pater noster* 20 *. . . et ne nos. Protector noster.* Oremus. *Adesto quesumus, Domine, Deus noster, et quos sancte crucis.* Þridde time alswa ant þe feorðe ant þe fifðe. Naut ne changeð bute þe salmes ant þe oreisuns. |fol.15ᵛ| Þe forme *Iubilate*, þoðer *Ad te leuaui*, þe þridde *Qui confidunt*, þe feorðe *Domine, non est exaltatum*, þe fifðe *Laudate Dominum in sanctis eius.* In euch an beoð fif uers. Þe fiue oreisuns beoð *Deus, qui sanctam crucem*; *Adesto*; *Deus, qui pro nobis Filium*; *Deus, qui vnigeniti Filii tui*; *Iuste Iudex*; wið *O, beata et intemerata.* Ant hwase ne ⟨con⟩ þeos fif vreisuns, segge eauer an, ant hwase þuncheð to long, leaue þe salmes. 30

⟨Of Ure Leafdi Fif Goiez⟩

"Leauedi Seinte Marie, for þilke muchele blisse þet þu hefdest

heart's chamber from heaven, and hold him warmly close until he has granted you all you wish.

Let her meditate, at about midday who can, or some time, on God's cross as much as she can and on his precious torment, and begin thereafter the same five greetings that are written above,[85] and also kneel at each one, and cross herself as indicated there, and beat her breast, and say such a prayer as this: *We adore you, O Christ. We adore your cross. . . . Hail, holy cross. Hail, cross, you who. . . . O cross, wood triumphant.*

Then let her arise and begin the antiphon *Save us, O Christ*,[86] and while standing say the psalm *O be joyful*[87] together with the *Glory be to the Father*, and then say the antiphon thus: *Save us, O Christ the savior, through the power of the holy cross*, and cross herself; then let her say *You who rescued Peter on the sea, have mercy upon us*,[88] and beat the breast, and then fall and say *O Christ, hear us. O Christ, hear us. Lord, have mercy upon us; Christ, have mercy upon us; Lord, have mercy upon us. Our Father . . . and lead us not into temptation. Our protector, God, look upon and see the face of your Christ.*[89] Let us pray. *God, who ascended the holy cross.*[90]

Thereafter, begin *We adore*, saying all five, as before; the antiphon *Save us, O Christ* as before; the psalm *I have lifted up to you*; and then the antiphon to the end; and then let her fall to the ground as before. Say *O Christ, hear us. Lord, have mercy upon us. Our Father . . . and lead us not into temptation. Our protector.* Let us pray. *We beseech you be present, O Lord, our God, and those you made rejoice in the honor of the holy cross.*[91] Repeat this sequence the third, fourth, and fifth times. Change nothing except the psalms and orisons. The first psalm is *O be joyful*, the second is *I have lifted up*, the third *Those who trust*,[92] the fourth *O Lord, my heart is not exalted*,[93] and the fifth *Praise the Lord in his sanctuaries.*[94] Each contains five verses. The five orisons are as follows: *God, who ascended the holy cross*;[95] *Be present*;[96] *God, who consented that your Son should suffer for us*;[97] *God, who with the precious blood of your only begotten Son*;[98] and *Righteous Judge.*[99] Recite with *O blessed and pure.*[100] Whoever does not know these five orisons may say the same one each time, and whoever thinks this too long may leave out the psalms.

## Of Our Lady's Five Joys

"O Lady, St. Mary,[101] because of the same great happiness that

in þé i þen ilke time þet Iesu God, Godes sune, efter þe en⟨g⟩les
gretunge nom flesch ant blod in þé ant of þé, vnderfeng mi
gretunge wið þet ilke *Aue*, ant make me telle lutel of uch blisse
utewið; ach freoure me inwið, ant erende me þe⟨o⟩ blissen,
⟨Lefdi⟩, of heoue⟨ne⟩, ant ase wis as in þilke flech þet ⟨he⟩ toc
⟨of þé⟩ nes neauer sunne ⟨in⟩ ne in þin, as me leueð efter þilke
tac⟨unge⟩, hwetse bifor were, clense mi saule of flesliche sunnen." *Aue Maria*; *Magnificat*; *Aue Maria*; al vt fif siðen.

|fol.16ʳ| "Leauedi Seinte Marie, for þilke muchele blisse þe
þu hefdest þa þu segʒe þilke blisfule bearn iboren of þine cleane   10
bodie to moncunne heale wiðvten eauer vh bruche wið hal
medenhad ant meidenes menske, heal me þet am þurch wil
tobroken, alse ich drede, hwetse beo of de⟨d⟩e; ant ʒef me in
heouene seon þi blisfule bearn ant bihalde þe meidene menske,
ʒef ich ⟨n⟩am wurðe to beon ⟨iblisset⟩ in heore ferredene." *Aue
Maria*; *Ad Dominum cum tribularer*; fif siðen.

"Leauedi Seinte Marie, for þe muchele blisse þet þu hefdest
þa þu sechʒe þi deorewurðe sune efter ⟨his⟩ derfe deað arisen to
blisfule li⟨f⟩, his bodi seouefald brichtere þenne þe sunne, ʒef me
deiʒe wið him ant arisen in him, worldliche deiʒen, gastliche lib-   20
ben, dealen wið his pinen feolaʒeliche in eorðe for to beon in
blisse his feolaʒe in heouene. For þilke muchele blisse þet þu
hefdest, Leauedi, of his blisful ariste efter |fol.16ᵛ| þin muchele
soreʒe, efter mi muchele soreʒe þet ich am in her, lead me to
þi blisse." *Aue Maria*; *Retribue*; fif siðen.

"Leauedi Seinte Marie, for þe muchele blisse þet þu hefdest
þa þu sechʒe þi blisfule sune, þet þe Gius wenden for to prisunen
in þruch, swa wurðliche ant michteliche on Hali Þuresdei
stiʒin[de] to his blisse, into his riche ⟨in⟩ heouen⟨e⟩, ʒef me warpe
wið him al þe world vnderfet ant stiʒe nu heortiliche; ⟨h⟩wenne   30
ich deiʒe, gastliche; an Domesdei, al licomliche to heouenliche
blisse." *Aue*; *In conuertendo*; fif siððen.

"Leauedi Seinte Marie, for þe muchele blisse þet fullede alle
⟨þe oþere⟩ þa he vnderfeng þé ⟨wið⟩ vnimete blisse ant wið hise
blisfule armes sette þé in trone ant ⟨cwenene⟩ crune ⟨sette þé⟩
on heaued brichtere þenne þe sunne, ⟨heʒe⟩ heouenliche quen,

you felt in yourself at the very time when Jesus God, son of God, after the angel's greeting, assumed your flesh and blood in you and of you, accept my greeting with the same *Hail Mary*, and make me place little value on every outward joy; but comfort me within and send me those joys of heaven, O Lady, and inasmuch as there was never sin in the same flesh that he took from you, nor in your own, as one believes according to the same token, whatever there may have been before, cleanse my soul of fleshly sins." Say five times in their entirety *Hail Mary*; *My soul magnifies the Lord*; *Hail Mary*.

"O Lady, St. Mary, because of the same great happiness that you had upon seeing the same blessed child born of your pure body for mankind's salvation without any breach of complete virginity and virgin's honor, heal me who am destroyed because of my will, I fear, whatever deeds I might perform; and permit me in heaven to see your blessed child and behold the praiseworthy virgins, although I am not worthy to be blessed in their ranks." Recite *Hail Mary* and *To the Lord when I was troubled*[102] five times.

"O Lady, St. Mary, because of the great happiness you had when you saw your precious son after his cruel death arise to the blessed life, his body sevenfold brighter than the sun, allow me to die with him and arise in him, to die in the world, to live in the spirit, to share as a companion on earth in his torments in order to be his fellow in heavenly bliss. Because of the same great happiness that you had in his blessed arising, O Lady, after your great sorrow, lead me to your bliss after my great sorrow that I am in here." Say *Hail Mary* and *Deal bountifully with your servant*[103] five times.

"O Lady, St. Mary, because of the great happiness that you had when you saw your blessed son, whom the Jews thought to imprison in a tomb, arising to his bliss, into his kingdom in heaven, so splendidly and mightily on Holy Thursday, allow me with him to cast all the world underfoot and ascend to heavenly bliss, in heart now, in spirit when I die, and fully in body on Judgment Day." Recite *Hail Mary* and *When the Lord restored again the fortunes of Zion*[104] five times.

"O Lady, St. Mary, because of your great happiness that completed all the others when he received you with unmeasured joy and with his blessed arms set you on the throne and placed a queen's crown on your head brighter than the sun, O high heavenly queen, accept these greetings from me thus on earth so that I may greet

vnderfeng þeose gretunges of me swa on eorðe, þet ich mote
blisfulliche grete þé in heoue⟨ne⟩." *Aue; Ad te leuaui;* fif siðen.
    Ant þenne þe uerset |fol.17ʳ| *Spiritus Sanctus superueniet in te;
et uirtus altissimi obumbrabit tibi.* Oremus. *Gratiam tuam.*
    Þenne þeos antefne:

> *Aue, Regina celorum*
> *Aue, Domina angelorum*
> *Salue, radix sancta,*
> *Ex qua mundo lux est orta.*
> ⟨*Aue, gloriosa*                                            10
> *Super omnes speciosa*⟩
> *Vale, ualde decora,*
> *Et pro nobis semper Cristum exora.*

    Verset: *Egredietur uirga de radice Iesse et flos de radice eius ascendet.*
Oremus. *Deus, qui uirginalem aulam.*
    Antiphona:

> *Gaude, Dei genitrix, Virgo immaculata.*
> *Gaude, que gaudium ab angelo suscepisti.*
> *Gaude, que genuisti eterni luminis claritatem.*
> *Gaude, Mater.*                                            20
> *Gaude, sancta Dei genitrix; Virgo, tu sola Mater innup-*
>      *ta. Te laudat omnis ⟨filii tui creatura⟩ genitricem lucis.*
>      *Sis pro nobis pia interuentrix.*

    Versiculus: *Ecce, in utero concipies et paries filium et uocabis nomen
eius Iesum.* Oremus. *Deus, qui de beate Marie semper. . . .*
    Antiphona:

> *Gaude, Virgo;*
> *Gaude, Dei genitrix;*
> *Et gaude, gaudium, Maria, omnium fidelium.*
> *Gaudeat ecclesia in tuis laudibus.*                       30
> *Assidua et pia Domina, gaudere fac nos tecum ante*
>      *Dominum.*

you blissfully in heaven." Recite *Hail Mary* and *To you I have lifted up my eyes,* [105] five times.

And then say the versicle *The Holy Spirit will come upon you and the power of the most high will overshadow you.* [106] Let us pray. *Pour forth your grace.* [107]

Then say this antiphon:

> *Hail, Queen of heaven.*
> *Hail, Ruler of angels.*
> *Hail, sacred source*
> *From which light has arisen on the world.*
> *Hail, glorious*
> *Beyond all beautiful things.*
> *Prevail, O most lovely one,*
> *And entreat Christ for us always.* [108]

Say this versicle: *There shall come forth a shoot from the root of Jesse and a flower shall grow out of his root.* [109] Let us pray. *God, who deigned to choose the virginal residence.* [110]

Say this antiphon:

> *Rejoice, Mother of God, immaculate Virgin.*
> *Rejoice, you who have received joy from the angel.*
> *Rejoice, you who have begotten the splendor of eternal light.*
> *Rejoice, O Mother.*
> *Rejoice, holy Mother of God; Virgin, you alone are pure*
> *    Mother and Virgin. Every creature of your son praises*
> *    you, Mother of light. Be for us a holy mediatrix.* [111]

Say this versicle: *Behold, you shall conceive in your womb and bear a son and call his name Jesus.* [112] Let us pray. *O God, who from the womb of the blessed Mary always. . . .* [113]

Say this antiphon:

> *Rejoice, O Virgin;*
> *Rejoice, Mother of God;*
> *And, Mary, joy of all the faithful, rejoice.*
> *Let the church rejoice in your praises.*
> *Constant and holy Lady, make us rejoice with you before*
> *    the Lord.* [114]

Versiculus: *Ecce, Virgo concipiet et pariet filium.* Oremus. *Deus, qui salutis.*
    Antiphona:


> *Alma Redemptoris Mater, que peruia celi*
> *Porta manes et* |fol.17ᵛ| *stella maris, sucurre cadenti*
> *Surgere qui curat populo; tu que genuisti*
> *Natura mirante tuum sanctum genitorem,*
> *Virgo prius ac posterius, Gabrielis ⟨ab⟩ ore*
> *Sumens illud Aue, peccatorum miserere.*


Her sitteð ⟨te seggen ower tale of *Avez*⟩, fifti oðer hundret, ma  10
oðer lees, efter ⟨þet ȝe wulleð⟩.
    On ende, þe uerset *Ecce, ancilla Domini. Fiat michi.* Oremus.
*O sancta ⟨Virgo uirginum⟩.*
    Hwase wule mei stutten þrupe anan richtes efter þe formeste
vreisun, *Gratiam tuam*, ant segge þenne hire tale of *Auees* efter
þe leste salm, *Ad te leuaui.* Eauer bifore þe salm biginnen an *Aue*,
oðet cume to *Dominus tecum*, ant segge stondinde þe salm. Þe
salmes beoð inumene efter þe fif letteres of Vre Lauedi nome,
hwase nimeð ȝeme, ant al þis ilke vreisun efter hire fif heste
blissen eorneð bi fiue. Tele in þe antefnes, ant þu schalt finden  20
in ham gretunges fiue. Þe oreisuns, þet ich nabbe bute an i-
marked, beoð iwriten ouer al, wiðuten þe leste. Leteð writen
on an scrouwe |fol.18ʳ| hwetse ȝe ne cunnen.
    Al þet ȝe eauer seggeð of þullich oðere bonen, as *Pater Nosteres*
ant *Auees*, on oure aȝen wise, ich am apaied. Of salmes ant
vreisuns vch an segge ase best bereð hire on heorte; versailunge
of Sauter, redunge of Englisch oðer of Frensch hali þochtes,
cneolunges, hwense ȝe maȝen iȝemen, ear mete ant efter. Eauer
se ȝe mare doð, se God ⟨echi ow⟩ forðere his grace. Ach lokeð
swa, ich bidde ou, þet ȝe ne beon neauer idel, ach wurchen oðer  30
reden oðer beon i beoden, ant swa don eauer sumþing þet god
maȝe of ⟨arisen⟩.
    Þe vres of þe Hali Gast, ȝef ȝe ham wulleð seggen, seggeð vch
tide of ham bifore Vre Lauedi tiden. Toward þe preostes tiden
hercnið se forð se ȝe maȝen, ach wið him ne schule ȝe nouðer
uersailen ne singgen þet he maȝe iheren.

Say this versicle: *Behold a virgin shall conceive and bear a son.*[115] Let
us pray. *God, who for our salvation.*[116]

Say the antiphon:

*Fruitful Mother of the Redeemer, you who remain the accessible*
*Gate to heaven and star of the sea, succor the stumbling people*
    *who seek*
*To rise; you who gave birth to your holy Father while*
*Nature looked on amazed;*
*Virgin before and after, from the mouth of Gabriel*
*Taking that Hail Mary, have mercy on sinners.*[117]

Now sit to say your sum of *Hail Marys*, fifty or a hundred, more
or less, as you wish.

Finally, say the versicle *Behold, I am the handmaid of the Lord. Let
it be to me according to your word.*[118] Let us pray. *O holy Virgin of
virgins.*[119]

Whoever wishes may stop immediately after *Pour forth your grace,*
the first prayer given above, and may say her *Hail Marys* after the
last psalm, *To you I have lifted.* Before the psalm she should always
begin a *Hail Mary*, until she comes to *the Lord is with you*, and she
should say the psalm standing. The psalms are selected according
to the five letters of Our Lady's name,[120] as whoever takes heed
will see, and all this same prayer concerning her five highest joys
goes in fives. Count in the antiphons, and in each of them you will
find five greetings. The prayers, which I have only noted, are written
everywhere, except for the last.[121] Have written on a scroll whatever
you do not know.

All that you ever say of other such prayers, as *Our Fathers* and
*Hail Marys*, in your own way, I am pleased with. Each of you may
say psalms and prayers, whichever ones you have best in mind;
attend to your singing of versicles, reading of holy meditations in
English or French, and your kneelings, before meat and after,
whenever you can. The more you do these things, so may God
further increase his grace toward you. But I urge you, take care
never to be idle, but work or read or be in prayer, and thus always
do something from which good can arise.

If you want to say the hours of the Holy Spirit,[122] say each of
them before the corresponding hour of Our Lady. Listen as much
as you can to the priest's singing of hours, but you must not recite
versicles or sing with him so that he hears you.

Ouwer graces stondinde, bifore mete ant effter, as heo beoð
iwritene ou, ant wið þe *Miserere* gað bifore |fol.18ᵛ| þe weoued,
ant endið þer ouwer graces. Bituewene mel þe drinke wule, segge
*Benedicite; potum nostrum Filius Dei benedicat; in nomine Patris*, ant
blesci. Efterward *Adiutorium nostrum in nomine. Sit nomen Domini
benedictum ex hoc. Benedicamus Domino. Deo gratias.*

Hwense ȝe gað to oure bedde, i nicht oðer in euen, falleð a-
cneon ant þencheð i hwat ȝe habbeð i dei iwraððet oure Lauerd,
ant crieð ȝeorne merci ant forȝeouenesse. Ȝef ȝe habbeð ani god
don, þonkeð him of his ȝeoue wiðvte hwam ȝe ne maȝe wel don   10
ne wel þenchen, ant seggeð *Miserere. Kirieleyson; Criste. Pater noster
. . . et ne nos. Saluos fac seruos tuos et ancillas tuas.* Oremus. *Deus,
cui proprium est misereri*; ant stondinde, *Uisita, Domine, habitacionem
istam*; ant þenne alest, *Cristus vincit* ✝ *Cristus regnat* ✝ *Cristus
inperat* ✝ , wið þreo crosses wið þe þume i ðe forheaued, ant
þenne *Ecce crucem Domini; fugite partes, aduerse; vicit leo de tribu Iuda,
radix Dauid; Alleluia*; an large croiz as ed *Deus, in adiutorium* wið
*Ecce crucem Domini*, ant þenne fouwer |fol.19ʳ| crosses a four half
wið þeos fouwer efter clauses:


*Crux* ✝ *fugat omne malum.*                              20
*Crux* ✝ *est reparacio rerum.*
*Per crucis* ✝ *hoc signum*
*Fugiat procul omne malignum,*
*Et per idem signum* ✝
*Saluetur quodque benignum.*


On ende on ouself ant on oure bed baðe. *In nomine Patris.* In
bedde ne do ȝe naut bute slepen.

Hwase ne con oðer vtsong segge þritti *Pater Nosteres* ant *Aue
Maria* efter vh an *Pater Noster* ant *Gloria Patri* efter vh *Aue Maria.*
Alast, hwase con, Oremus. *Deus, cui proprium est misereri*;   30
*Benedicamus Patrem et Filium; Anime fidelium.* For euensong twen-
ti, for vh oðer tide segge fiftene on þisse wise; buten ed vtsong
he schal seggen earest, hwase con, *Domine, labia mea aperies* ant
*Deus, in adiutorium*; ant ed compeli *Conuerte, Deus* ant *Deus, in
adiutorium.* Hwase is vnheite, forcorue tene of vtsong, of vh oðer

Say your graces standing, before and after eating, as they are written for you, and at *Lord have mercy* go before the altar and there finish your graces. Let whoever wants to drink between meals say *Benedicite; may the son of God bless our drink; in the name of the Father,* [123] and make the sign of the cross. Afterward say *Our help is in the name of the Lord. Blessed be the name of the Lord from this time forth and forevermore. Let us bless the Lord. Thanks be to God.* [124]

Whenever you go to bed, at night or in the evening, fall to your knees and think in what ways you have angered our Lord during the day, and sincerely cry out for mercy and forgiveness. If you have done any good, thank him, without whom you can neither do nor think well, for his gift, and say *Have mercy. Lord have mercy; Christ have mercy. Our Father . . . and lead us not into temptation. Save your servants and your handmaidens.* Let us pray. *God, whose property is always to have mercy;* and standing say *Visit, O Lord, this house;* [125] and then, finally, *Christ conquers* ✛ *Christ is king* ✛ *Christ rules* [126] ✛, making three crosses on the forehead with the thumb, and then say *Behold the cross of the Lord; flee, enemy; the lion of the tribe of Judah, the root of David, has conquered; Alleluia.* [127] At *Behold the cross of the Lord* make a large cross as at *God, come to our aid* [128] and then four crosses on four sides, while saying these next four sentences:

> The cross ✛ drives away all evil.
> The cross ✛ is the restorer of things.
> By this sign of the cross ✛
> May all evil flee far away,
> And by the same sign ✛
> May whatever is good be preserved. [129]

At last make the sign of the cross both on yourself and on your bed. Say *In the name of the Father.* Do nothing but sleep in your bed.

Whoever does not know other matins may say thirty *Our Fathers* and *Hail Mary* after each *Our Father* and *Glory be to the Father* after each *Hail Mary.* At the last, for those who know it, let us pray. *God, whose property is always to have mercy; Let us bless the Father and the Son;* and *The souls of the faithful.* At evensong say twenty, at every other hour say fifteen in this fashion, except that at matins whoever can must say first *O Lord, open my lips* and *God, come to our aid;* and at compline *Turn, O God* and *God, come to our aid.* Whoever is unwell may cut ten from matins and five from every other hour; whoever

tide fiue, þe haluendal hwase is sekere. ⟨Al seke beoð al cwite⟩.
Neomeð oure secnesse þolemodliche ant gledliche, ant þencheð
mest in ouwer tiden of God, |fol.19ᵛ| þet ouwer þochtes ne beon
fleotinde þenne.

Ʒef ʒe þurch ʒemeles gluffeð of wordes oðer misneomeð uers,
neomeð ouwer *Venie* dun et þeorðe wið þe hond ane, ant al fallen
adun for muche misneominge, and schawið ofte ed schrifte ouwer
ʒemeles herabuten.

Þis is nu þe forme dale, þet haueð ispeken hiderto of ouwer
seruise. Hwetse beo nu þerof þeos riulen herefter, ich walde ha 10
weren ⟨of⟩ alle ⟨oþre⟩ as ha beoð ⟨onond ow⟩ þurch Godes grace
ihalden.

is more ill may cut half. The extremely ill are excused from all. Take your illness patiently and gladly, and meditate most about God during your hours so that your thoughts are not wandering then.

If through heedlessness you blunder over words or mistake a verse, say your *Pardon* with only your hands on the ground, and prostrate yourself entirely for great mistakes, and reveal often in confession your carelessness in this respect.

Now this is the first part, which has spoken of your service. Whatever more beyond this there may now be of these rules, I would wish that they were kept by all others as they are, with God's grace, by you.

# Textual Notes

The textual notes are keyed to page and line numbers. Brackets in the text are not repeated in the lemmata. After the lemmata, Middle English or Latin text not preceded by a notation is Scribe A's as it stood before B revised it. When the edited text diverges from the manuscript, the manuscript reading is supplied, preceded by the notation *MS*. *A* = Cleopatra Scribe A, *B* = Cleopatra Scribe B, *Cor* = MS Corpus Christi College Cambridge 402, *Dobs* = E. J. Dobson's edition of MS British Library Cotton Cleopatra C. VI, and *F* = Herbert's edition of MS British Library Cotton Vitellius F. VII. Square brackets enclose Dobson's reconstructions of manuscript text. Parentheses enclose editorial comments.

42:4 **grammaticum**] *MS gramaticum; Dobs grammaticum.*    9 **beoð richte**] beoð [þe] richte | **ant ȝe**] (*A*'s text irrecoverable).    10 **icraued me**] icraued [on] me.    13-14 **woh . . . segge**] þoncg inwið, unwrest, ant ȝirninde þet þu.    20 **unefne**] *Dobs* uilefne (reading blotted "un" as "uil").    25 **als a**] als[w]a.
44:6-7 **inwit . . . hireseoluen**] inwið wiðvten weote of sunne.    9 **þe inwit aȝein**] wit hire from.    10 **makeð**] *MS* marreð | **woh, scraggi, ant unefne**] þong (for "wrong"); *F* tort.    19 **istalt**] nis heo italt.    38 **bihaten heste alswa ase heste**] *F* promettre ausi come comandement.    39 **studeuestnesse**] studestaðeluestninge.
46:6 **brekeð**] breket.    12 **bihoten**] forhoten.    14 **alle þe**] þe alde.    16 **beoð naut**] beoð þeose naut.    17 **Godes hestes**] Godes Godes hestes.    18 **alle**] alle þinge | **þe**] ðe.    19 **i**] i[n] | **i**] i[n].    20 **þer of þe**] þerof [in] þe[t].    24 **breken eni of ham**] bre[o]ke[ð] an þerof | **walde**] hurteð.    25 **maken**] makeð | **offered**] offe[a]red | **muhten**] muȝe.    26 **i desesperance, þet is, inte**] in (not cancelled by *B*).    35 **icleoped**] *Dobs* icleopet.    38 **þet is**] *F* Cest.    40 **wem is**] wem[e]s [to].
48:2 **Iame**] Iame[s].    4 **religiuse**] religiun.    7 **Iame**] Iame[s].    10 **federles**] *Dobs* federlese.    13 **Iame**] Iame[s].    15 **Iame**] *MS* Iames.    17 **makeð muche**] makeð [strengðe] muche.    20 **þe oþre hali men sumhwile**] þoðe.    22 **Sincletece**] Sinc[h]ete.    25 **þe weneð**] [h]e weneð.    26 **spuse**] *MS* spuses.    29 **ordre: þet**] ordre | **beoð**] *MS* beod; *Dobs* beoð.    30 **Sein**] *Dobs* Seint.    34 **for**] for[e].    39 **of**] as.
50:3 **oðer wummon**] [ant] mimmon.    4 **ham**] him.    5 **scandle**] schonde

| cume] come.    10 wac euer þeseoluen] as þeseolf.    11 dred] dreed.
13 wiðute] [ant] | trichunge] So *Cor;* *MS* trichi; *Dobs* tr[u]ch[unge] (*B* is
possibly responsible for erasing the second minim of *A*'s "u" to make
"trichunge"; the erasure marks before the "c" are characteristic of *B*'s work
in that they extend below the line, but otherwise the alterations to the word
are characteristic of Scribe D; see *Dobs,* p. 12, n. 8, and p. liv).    14 oðer]
*MS* oðe | efter] e[f]fter.    15 tole] (*B* glosses "lome").    23-24 desting-
ciun] destingciuns.    **54:5 heouene]** *MS* heoue.    6 imne vt mit] imne vt al mit.    9 Fili] *MS*
*Filii.*    10 a þet] a eauermor ad.    12 sitte] sitte[n].    20 nostre expec-
tacionis] *nostre redempcionis expectacionis.*    24 cuncta] *MS* cunta.
**56:4 hit]** hire.    5 hwen] hwenne.    7 þe vif wunden] þe vif wunden of
Gode.    13 preciosum] *MS precium.*    17 O] (*B* erases and corrects
rubricator's capital "G") | triumphale] *triumphate.*    25 Sit in] *Sine.*    28
cusseð] cusset.    30 onlicnesse] *MS* onlitnesse (*B* suffixes "se" but allows
"t" to stand).
**58:4 duneward]** *MS* duneward ant (*B* incorrectly inserts "ant") | ant Credo]
*MS* ant ant *Credo.*    7 breoste] *MS* beoste.    9-10 biginnunge] *Dobs* begin-
nunge.    11 hwerse ȝe eauer hereð] So *Cor;* *F* ou qe vous orrez; *MS* hwerse
hereð.    22 ed ex Maria] So *Cor;* *F* a cest mot *ex Maria; MS ex Maria.*
26 þis] Þe.    30 Non] Naut.    34 þe oþer] þoð.
**60:10 Requiem]** *Requiam.*    11 dona . . . sitteð] ant *Placebo* seoðen.    12
asswa] asswo.    13 stondeð] *MS* stonden (see *Dobs,* p. 21, n. k).    26
þoðer] MS þoð | ne nos] *MS ne ne nos.*    27 et . . . tuis] *etc.*    30 inferi
. . . eorum] *inferi* (*B* adds *inferi . . . eorum* in margin, but fails to delete *A*'s
*inferi*).    34 ant ibenen] þenne.
**62:6 michte]** *MS* wisdom; *Cor* mihte (*F* 's corresponding text lost).    8 þu an
almihti] aa michti[n].    14 ifeȝet] imenged.    15 i þe] iðe.    18 oðer sum
oðer] *MS* oðer sum (*A* mistakenly deletes second "oðer"); *F* ke lad ou ascun
altre oroison.    20 honged o] honge[ð] o[n þe].    22 al . . . þurh]
sun[ne]fule deden þet eauer is iwunden þorch.    28 slepe ic oðer wakie]
slepinde oðer wakinde.    34 Domine, etc.] *Deus.*    38 iteoheðet] itouðet.
**64:4 ase Seint Powel seið]** (*B* glosses *Ad Corinthios: Caritas patiens est, etc.*).
9 ow on] ower.    10 þermid] þet mid.    18 fouwer marheȝeuen] (*B* glosses
*quattuor dotes*).    19 ant . . . seggeð] ant seggeð (*Dobs* omits *B*'s "ant," beginning the addition with "ȝef," p. 26, n. h).    22 wulleð] *MS* wulled.    24
nihcte] *Dobs* nichte.    24-25 gederið . . . ant] þencheð vpoðe seke ant þe.
25 sarie, þe] sarie in oure heorte, þe | wa . . . pinen] [o þet þolieð þe
pine].    26 þolieð] doð.    29 sares] sares[t].    30 him neome] he nume.
**66:5 precium]** *MS premium.*    9 futurus] *Dobs futurum.*    19 Miserere] *MS*
*Misere* | loquar. Angusta] *MS loquar. Angustia est. Angusta.*    21 offendant]
*MS ostendant.*    28 quem enigmatice] *MS qem evingmatice.*    32 hwen]
hwen[ne].
**68:7 blesci]** *MS* blescin.    8 make] *MS* maken | a] [e]a[uer].    10 antefne]
antempne.    11 antefne] antempne.    12 saluator, per] *saluator mundi per*

| **blesci**] *MS* blescin.     **18 antefne**] antempne.     **19 antefne**] *MS* antempne.     **28 intemerata**] *MS intermerata*; *Dobs intemerata*.     **31 Goiez**] *Dobs* goies.
**70:4 blissen**] *MS* blisse.     **5 he**] þe.     **7 tacunge**] tacnunge.     **8 Maria; al vt**] *Maria*; *Magnificat* al vt.     **10 segȝe**] (*B* glosses "sehe").     **13 dede**] deðe.     **15 iblisset**] in blisse.     **18 his**] þeos.     **19 lif**] li[ue].     **24 mi**] mi[n].     **25 þi**] þi[n].     **26 Leauedi Seinte**] *MS* Leauedi Seinte Seinte.     **29 in**] to.     **32 conuertendo**] *MS conuertando*.     **33 þe**] (or "þilke"; the manuscript abbreviation can be expanded either way; *Dobs*, p. 32, n. 11).     **34 þe oþere**] þeode.     **35 cwenene**] cuwene.     **36 heȝe**] hechȝe.
**72:3 superveniet**] *MS supervениat*.     **5 antefne**] *MS* antempne.     **22 filii tui creatura**] *creatura filii tui* (*B* puts transposition marks around *A*'s text).     **23 pia interuentrix**] *MS pia perpetua interuentrix* (the *perpetua*, apparently a mistake, inserted by *B*).
**74:10 te . . . Avez**] *Auez*.     **11 þet ȝe wulleð**] wil haldeð.     **13 Virgo uirginum**] *uirginum Virgo* (*B* puts transposition marks around *A*'s text).     **20 antefnes**] *MS* antempnes.     **21-22 bute an imarked**] *Cor* buten ane i-mearket; *F* merchee fors vne soule; *MS* imarked bute an.     **29 echi ow**] echeð.     **31 god**] (*B* adds diacritic, altering the meaning from "good" to "God").     **32 arisen**] wacnen.     **35 schule ȝe nouðer**] *Cor* schule ȝe nowðer; *F* ne deuez vou; *MS* schule nouðer.
**76:5 blesci**] *MS* blescin.     **8 i hwat**] *Cor* i hwet; *F* en quei; *MS* hwat.     **11 Criste**] *Dobs* Cristeleyson.     **12 ne nos. Saluos**] *MS ne. Saluos*.
**78:2 þolemodliche**] *Dobs* þolemodeliche.     **11 of**] þurch.

# Explanatory Notes

# Explanatory Notes

An explanation of the abbreviated titles appearing in the notes and elsewhere is incorporated into the Bibliography. Psalms are referred to in accordance with the numbering in the Vulgate Bible. Only the notes pertaining to the many liturgical forms usually indicated in *AR* by no more than a short Latin cue call for additional comment. The primary objective of such notes is to direct the reader to the full medieval texts of the prayers, hymns, antiphons, and other formulas as they are given in available service books of the Middle Ages, chiefly breviaries. An observation about the common liturgical setting of the form in question is included when appropriate, and care is taken to point out that many forms occur in the eleventh-century texts of the Office of Our Lady, edited by E. S. Dewick (see Bibliography under *Facsimiles*.)

## Notes to General Introduction

1. Shepherd, ed., *Ancrene Wisse, Parts Six and Seven*, p. lx. In the present edition, the style *Ancrene Riwle* (*AR*) is chosen over *Ancrene Wisse* despite the claim of the latter to greater authenticity, deriving from its appearance as the title in one manuscript (C. C. C. C. 402). See Magoun; also E. J. Dobson, "The Date and Composition of *Ancrene Wisse*," p. 181; *Origins of AW*, pp. 51–3. On the other hand, *Ancrene Riwle* is used as the title of each of the editions of the various texts issued by the Early English Text Society. Moreover, the word *riwle*, of much more frequent occurrence than *wisse* in the English forms of the work, is immediately recognizable to the modern reader. *Ancrene* is preferred to *ancren* because, as noted by Magoun, the inflectional -*e*, representing the genitive plural, is a feature of early Middle English.

2. There are exceptions. Barbara Raw identifies and provides excellent comments on a number of the incipits, in particular private prayers and devotions to the cross. Our indebtedness to her work is acknowledged in the appropriate notes to Part I. In her unpublished Ph.D. dissertation,

Sister Ethelred Cooper treats very competently the Latin material used throughout *AR*, including the liturgical incipits in Part I. She does not as a rule specify the common settings of the liturgical forms, as is done here, but we are indebted to her work for several suggestions, as our notes to Part I indicate, and we are grateful to her for permission to include these citations. Also unpublished, Glenys Magee's M.A. thesis concentrates on Part I of *AR*, but in liturgical matters it is largely derivative of Sister Ethelred's dissertation. In an appendix to the Salu translation of *AR*, Dom Gerard Sitwell provides a general discussion of the private devotions (Salu, pp. 193–96). In his inquiry into the date of composition of *AR*, Talbot provides valuable background on certain liturgical forms. See also Ackerman, "The Liturgical Day in *Ancrene Riwle*."

3. Schofield (p. 403) calls the author "a truly lovable old man."

4. Humphrey Wanley, in his portion of Hickes's *Thesaurus*, describes several of the *AR* manuscripts. He regarded the Middle English work, to which he refers as *Ancrene Wisse*, as a translation from the Latin of Simon of Ghent, bishop of Salisbury (1298–1315). See Hickes, 2: 149, 228, and 247. Sir Frederic Madden, Keeper of Manuscripts in the British Museum (1827–1866), states in his unpublished diary under the date 25 November 1835 that he was again reading "the rule for recluses or nuns" of the reign of Henry III in three manuscripts of the Cottonian Collection. He had earlier inspected the Latin version in Magdalen College, Oxford. Among the first scholars to comment on Morton's edition of 1853, Madden supported Morton's view that the language of the original rule was English and that the age of the manuscripts precluded authorship by Simon of Ghent. He further considered MS Cotton Cleopatra C.VI to provide the earliest copy. See his " 'The Ancren Riwle.' "

5. In his preface (p. xvii), Morton speaks of the English author's style as "plain, unambitious." Some half century later, Schofield (p. 97), under the impression that the author was Richard Poore, compared the perfection of his prose style to the architectural perfection of Bishop Poore's Salisbury Cathedral. In *The Cambridge History of English Literature* (1: 255), *AR* is called "the greatest prose work of the time" and "one of the most interesting of the whole Middle English period." R. W. Chambers, in "Recent Research," p. 4, justified his interest in the work on the grounds that "the Rule is the greatest book of its class in either Anglo-Norman or English."

6. Chambers, *On the Continuity of English Prose*, pp. xcvi–c. Grayson, *Structure and Imagery*. See further a number of unpublished dissertations, such as those of Hastings and Felperin.

7. Rejecting Wanley's belief in Simon of Ghent's authorship, Morton argued for an earlier bishop of Salisbury, Richard Poore. In 1916, Fr. Vincent McNabb, O.P., repeated a predecessor's contention that the Rule was the work of a Dominican friar. At about the same time, Hope Emily Allen sought to associate *AR* with three women to whom the hermitage

of Kilburn was granted between 1127 and 1135. Though impressively set forth, this argument fails because it is founded on too early a date of composition. These and similar conjectures are reviewed in Chambers' "Recent Research" and the Introduction to Shepherd's edition of Parts VI and VII, pp. xxi-xxv. In a more recent study, *The Origins of Ancrene Wisse*, E. J. Dobson argues that the work was composed in Herefordshire at Wigmore, an Augustinian abbey of the Victorine congregation. He places the anchorhold of the original three sisters at Limebrook Priory, near Wigmore, and speculates that the author was their brother, Brian of Lingen, who reveals his name in a cryptogram.

8. See, for example, Grayson; Allen.

9. Charlotte D'Evelyn in Severs, p. 650.

10. In 1893, Bramlette sought to revive Wanley's notion of a Latin original, and two decades later Macaulay presented his evidence for positing a French original. In 1924, Dorothy Dymes published an argument for English as the first language, a position more recently refined and buttressed by Samuels and by Käsmann.

11. Dobson, "The Date and Composition," pp. 181-93, and also Dobs., pp. ix-xi.

12. See Shepherd's Introduction, *Ancrene Wisse*, pp. xiv-xxi. The "AB dialect" is so called because it is the dialect of MS C. C. C. C. 402 (MS "A") and MS Bodley 34 (MS "B"). Dobs., p. xviii.

13. Dobs., pp. xviii and xlvi-clxxiii.

14. Ed. Herbert. See Dobs., pp. x-xi, lvii-lxi.

15. "There can be little doubt that in the thirteenth century the Cleopatra MS was especially valued, and as its text is not especially good, owing to the deficiencies of the original scribe, it seems probable that it was esteemed because it was known to have been corrected by the author himself." Dobs., p. xi.

16. Ed. Tolkien. See Dobson, "Date and Composition," pp. 192 ff., esp. 206, and Dobs., pp. ix, cxvi ff., esp. cxxv.

17. Dobs., pp. xii, cxl-clxxii.

18. *An Anglo-Saxon Dictionary*, s.v. ancra, etc.

19. *Middle English Dictionary*, s.v. ancre, etc.

20. *The Oxford English Dictionary*, s.v. anchor, anchoret, anchorite, etc.

21. MacKean, pp. 76 ff.; O'Leary, pp. 22-31; Montalembert, 1:213ff.; and Waddell, pp. 4, passim. The biblically based symbolism of the wilderness is discussed by Williams, pp. 10-64. On the "hairy anchorite" and his relationship to the medieval "wild man" tradition, see Doob, pp. 160 ff. For a study of the early applications of the terms anchorite, monk, hermit, and the like, see Leclercq, pp. 1-28, 30, 98-100, etc.

22. Steele, p. 7; Darwin, pp. 15-16; Clay, pp. 128-45; MacKean, pp. 76-7.

23. *Butler's Lives of the Saints*, 1:19, 93, 140; 4:32; also O'Leary, pp. 22-31, and alphabetically, pp. 60-286.

24. Gougaud, *Dévotions*, pp. 175–94. See also *Butler's Lives of the Saints*, passim; *New Catholic Encyclopedia*, 4:895, s.v. *Discipline, The.*

25. Montalembert, 1:285 ff.

26. *Benedicti Regula*, pp. 17–19; Delatte, pp. 25–34.

27. Darwin, pp. 1–5; Clay, p. xvii.

28. Darwin, p. 5. Of relatively late date is the "Rule of Hermits of Cambridge," ed. Oliger, pp. 299 ff. Gougaud in *Ermites*, p. 6, quotes an "officium induendi et benedicendi heremitam" from the pontifical of Edmond Lacy (d. 1455).

29. Gougaud, *Ermites*, esp. Chap. 2, "Ermites clercs, ermites laïques," pp. 8 ff., and Chap. 6, "Vrais et faux ermites," pp. 42 ff.

30. Steele, p. 7; Gougaud, *Ermites*, pp. 66, 70.

31. Ed. Holthausen, p. 73. Cited in the *Middle English Dictionary*, s.v. ancre. In the same passage of *Vices and Virtues*, we are told that the hermit should not undertake life in the wilderness until tested by the rule—that is, by life in the cloister.

32. Clay, pp. xix, 73 ff., and Darwin, p. 8.

33. Grimlaic, esp. Chaps. 9–17, 25, 34–9, 42.

34. Wilmart, "Ève et Goscelin," pp. 42–83, esp. 69–75.

35. Ailred, *De Institutis Inclusarum*. See also Powicke, pp. xxxiii–lxviii, xcix–c.

36. Oliger, pp. 156–57.

37. Oliger, pp. 170–90. See esp. pp. 173, 175–80.

38. Clay, pp. 73–84, together with illustrations. Steele, pp. 217–51, is less satisfactory. See also Cook, pp. 205–06.

39. Clay, pp. 74–75. Clay provides further a tabulation of cells and of names of anchorites taken from historical records running from the seventh through the sixteenth century (Appendix C, pp. 203–63).

40. See, for example, Baugh, pp. 229–30. The standard survey of English writers of religious guides is Charlotte D'Evelyn's "Instructions for Religious," Pt. VI of Severs, pp. 458–81.

41. Russell, p. 212, Table 9, note a.

42. An office *Ad includendam anchoritam* from Bishop Lacy's pontifical is given in Steele, pp. 252–55, and a similar office from the Use of Sarum appears in translation in Clay, pp. 193–98. An historiated capital depicting the enclosure of an anchorite is reproduced from a fourteenth-century manuscript in Wordsworth and Littlehales, opp. p. 223. Gougaud (*Ermites*, pp. 66–75) surveys various rites of enclosure.

43. Most of the indications as to the anchoress's cell are gleaned from Pt. I of *AR*, but a few additional details may be inferred from remarks in the later "distinctions," especially Pt. VIII.

44. Liturgical references and ecclesiastical terms occurring in Pt. I are explained in notes to that portion of the text.

45. One folio containing the ending of Pt. VII and the opening of Pt.

VIII is missing from the Cleopatra manuscript. The first sentence of this summary is taken from other texts.

46. On the custom of the pittance and the monastic diet, see Knowles, pp. 463–64.

47. Grayson treats the structural implications of this passage, pp. 8 ff.

48. For a brief survey of such doctrinal treatises, see Ackerman, "*The Debate of the Body and the Soul*," esp. pp. 545–49.

49. See Gray, pp. 93 ff.

50. A statement in the Introduction seems to indicate that the author planned from the outset to include treatments of confession, penance, and charity as part of the inner rule (Fol. 6r).

51. Darwin, pp. 35–36.

52. The expressions "liturgical practices" and "liturgy" denote the worship officially organized by the Church, consisting primarily of the Mass and the Divine Office. Dix, pp. 1, 326–8.

53. "The monastic office was the first to have been organized on a complete and daily basis, with each member of the community personally obliged to take part. The basic texts are those of the Rule of St. Benedict." Salmon, p. 5.

54. St. Benedict provided no specific directions concerning the Mass when writing his rule, even though it was always the chief element of the liturgy. In English abbeys, two masses intended for the whole community were celebrated daily, the chapter or "morrow" mass and the later conventual high mass. In addition, monks in priest's orders celebrated privately. Knowles, pp. 468–69.

55. *Benedicti Regula*, Prologue, pp. 8–9; Chaps. 16, 17, 18. Knowles, p. 5.

56. *Benedicti Regula*, Chap. 16. In *The Leofric Missal*, p. 58, appears an interesting *horologium*, schematically presented. By means of six circles, each consisting of four rings, the diagram indicates how the proper time of day for celebrating the hours terce, none, and sext throughout the year may be calculated by measuring the length of a man's shadow. The editor calls attention to a similar *horologium* in MS Cotton Titus D. XXVII, fol. 12v.

57. St. Benedict used the older names "vigils" for the office before dawn, and "matins" for modern "lauds" (*Benedicti Regula*, Chaps. 12, 13). Even by Benedict's time the final psalms of the latter office (Pss. 148, 149, and 150) had come to be known as "lauds" because of the occurrence in each of *laudate* or *laudent*, and the term was eventually extended to include the entire office. Ultimately the term "matins" displaced "vigils" for the early devotions. *New Catholic Encyclopedia*, s.v. Matins, Lauds. (R. D.)

58. Tol., p. 173. Also, Knowles, pp. 448 ff. and *New Catholic Encyclopedia*, s.v. Compline, for further discussion of monastic practice.

59. See Knowles, pp. 448 ff., and Tol., pp. 152 ff.

60. A history of English monastic breviaries is outlined in Tol., pp. 1–7; Salmon, p. 12. Also, Batiffol.

61. Beginning as early as the tenth century, the clergy staffing many of the cathedral churches, all of which clergy were at that time seculars, came to adopt a monastic rule until the cathedrals in ten of the seventeen dioceses of thirteenth-century England were served by monastic chapters. Knowles, p. 133. Similarly, large collegiate churches, such as Ripon and St. George's, Windsor, were staffed by a "college" of clergy. Moorman, p. 19.

62. On canonical practice, Salmon, pp. 12–13. On the several Uses, Wordsworth and Littlehales, pp. 5–8 and passim; *The Sarum Missal*, p. v. The text of the Sarum canonical hours is given in *Sar. B.*

63. Salmon, pp. 1–27; on the imposition of the requirements on all secular priests, p. 9.

64. The Breviary obligation was made incumbent on all clerics in major orders, whether regulars or seculars, and also on simple monks, nuns, and "beneficiaries," or those who, even if only in minor orders, derived their living from the Church. *Codex Iuris Canonici*, can. 135, 610. It must be remembered that in the earlier medieval monasteries relatively few monks were in priest's orders. The proportion of priests increased gradually. Probably by the tenth century in England most monks proceeded to orders. Delatte, p. 413. See also Knowles, pp. 19, 468 ff.

65. Knowles, pp. 29–30, 148, 539 ff.

66. Knowles, p. 378.

67. *Reg. Con.* See especially Dom Thomas Symons' Introduction, pp. xxxi–xliv, and Knowles, pp. 42–5.

68. Grimlaic, Chaps. 24, 35.

69. Wilmart, "Ève et Goscelin," p. 72.

70. Ailred, Chap. 9.

71. Oliger, Chap. 18.

72. *Horae* or books of hours, which began to appear in the eleventh century, served a purpose somewhat analogous to that of the breviary for devout lay people. The core of the "hours" was the little Office of Our Lady, but in addition it commonly included a liturgical calendar, Gospel passages, the Seven Penitential Psalms, the Fifteen Gradual Psalms, the Litany of the Saints, the Office of the Dead, *memoriae* of the cross, and other special prayers. The Office of the Holy Ghost was of less frequent occurrence. In the fourteenth and fifteenth centuries magnificently illuminated "hours" were executed for royalty and great noblemen, but less elaborate books were produced in large numbers. The term "prymer" was applied especially to English translations, which were in use early in the fourteenth century. See *Prymer*, esp. the Introduction by Bishop, 109:lv ff.

73. Our purpose here is to outline the format of the devotions in *AR* and, in the notes to our edition of Pt. I, to direct the reader to medieval texts of the prayers, antiphons, hymns, and other forms indicated by the author of *AR* only by Latin incipits.

74. *Facs.*, pp. ix–xix, esp. xvi–xvii.

75. See note 72 above.

76. *Facs.*, pp. xi ff.

77. Knowles, pp. 448 ff. See also the summer and winter *horaria* in *Reg. Con.*, pp. xliii–xliv. The fact that the anchoresses of *AR* are advised to listen whenever possible to the "priest's hours" suggests that they were not bound to the recitation of the Divine Office but only to the Office of Our Lady.

78. See Dom Gerard Sitwell in Salu, pp. xxi–xxii, 193–196.

79. Fols. 14v–16v. On the history of the veneration of the cross, see Wilmart, "L'Office du crucifix."

80. The doctrine indicated by this expression, a variant of which is *opus operatum*, is that sacramental grace is conferred in the act of partaking of the sacraments. Jungmann, 1: 193, and *New Catholic Encyclopedia*, s.v. Sacraments.

81. This hypothetical *horarium* should be compared with the monastic day as outlined by Knowles, "The Monastic Horarium." The liturgical terms used here are explained in the notes to *AR*, Pt. I. Admittedly, even a thoughtful and devout recitation of the hours would occupy less time than the monastic office chanted in choir with accompanying ceremonial. Yet a reading of the full text of the anchoress's devotions will justify the estimate of the number of prayer hours given here.

## *Notes to AR: Introduction*

1. *In canticis. Canticum Canticorum Salomonis*, or Song of Solomon 1:3. The first two paragraphs of *AR* are marked by word play on the various senses of *rectus, regula, direccio, rectificacio, richte,* and *riwle*. The root meaning of these etymologically and semantically related words is "straight" and is the basis for the contrast in the second paragraph between the righted and the crooked conscience. Baldwin, p. 277. (R. D.)

2. *Seint Iames Pistel.* The Epistle of St. James 1:27.

3. *Pauwel þe earest ancre.* St. Paul (d. 342), a Desert Father, often called the first hermit. See General Introduction.

4. *Antonie.* St. Anthony (d. 356), a Desert Father.

5. *Arsenie.* St. Arsenius the Great (d. ca. 450), a Roman who as a monk in Egypt acquired a reputation for sanctity. *Butler's Lives of the Saints*, 19 July.

6. *Macarie.* St. Macarius, one of two fourth-century Desert Fathers of this name. Perhaps St. Macarius of Alexandria (d. 394), noted for his austerities, is intended here.

7. *Sarre.* Sarah, wife of Abraham, was regarded in the Middle Ages as a type of the Virgin. *New Catholic Encyclopedia*, s.v. Virgin.

8. *Sincletece.* St. Syncletia (d. ca. 400), a woman of Greek parentage who became a holy recluse in Egypt. *Butler's Lives of the Saints*, 5 Jan.

9. *Nigra sum sed formosa.* Song of Solomon 1:4. Used as an antiphon in Lauds of Our Lady. *Facs.*, 6.

10. *Michee þe Prophete.* Micah 6:8.

11. *destincciuns.* Adapted from Latin *distinctiones*, a university word. The author immediately translates this technical vocabulary by the less daunting, native *dalen* "parts." Geoffrey Shepherd, p. xxxviii. (R. D.)

12. *Daui in þe Sauter.* Ps. 101:6-7, which, however, mentions only three kinds of birds. Other texts of *AR* speak at this point of only one of the birds included in this psalm.

## Notes to AR: Part I

1. The sign of the cross and an invocation of the Trinity immediately upon awakening seems to have been established monastic custom. Tol., p. 56.

2. *Veni, Creator Spiritus.* A very famous breviary hymn still extensively used. Mone, 1: 241-43. For translation and commentary, see Britt, pp. 153-57. Also Szövérffy, 1:220-1; Raby, p. 183. First assigned to vespers, this hymn came generally to be used in terce since it celebrates the descent of the Holy Spirit, associated with the third hour. It was also used as a preparatory prayer for Mass. *Sar. B.*, 1:mviii-mix; 2:481. See also Wilmart, *Auteurs spirituels*, pp. 37-45.

3. *Emitte spiritum tuum.* Ps. 103:30. Commonly used as a versicle following *Veni, Creator Spiritus*, as in *Sar. B.*, 2:481. It also appears in Lauds of Our Lady, *Facs.*, 25.

4. *Deus, qui corda fidelium.* Prayer to the Holy Spirit which in its complete form begins *Deus, qui hodierna die corda fidelium*. Used at the conclusion of lauds at Pentecost (*Sar. B.*, 1:mviii), and in the "Westminster Missal" (2:1112) it follows the versicle *Emitte spiritum tuum* as here in *AR*.

5. *Credo in Deum.* The Apostles' Creed, which as early as the twelfth century was used in various of the hours following the *Pater Noster*. Tol., pp. 49-50.

6. *Iesu Criste, Fili Dei uiui.* Passages perhaps from this prayer appear as versicle and response in Prime of the Sarum Use. *Sar. B.*, 2:51. *Sar. B.*, Corpus, and the French text of Vitellius read *nobis* for Cleopatra *nostri*. (R. D.)

7. *Heȝe weoued.* The high altar of the church, visible to the anchoress through the "squint" in her cell.

8. *Aue principium nostre creacionis.* After *expectacionis* Corpus reads *Ave solamen nostre sustentationis.* Prayer or hymn of a type used at the elevation of the host. Mone, 1:292-3. In his discussion of the date of *AR*, C. H. Talbot identified this prayer as one attributed by Peter of Roissy (d. by 1213) to a *dominus P. Cancellarius Parisiensis*, either Peter of Poitiers (Chancellor, 1193-1204) or Praepositinus (Chancellor, 1206-10). Talbot,

pp. 49–50. It is worth observing that the identification, although no longer considered crucial for dating *AR* (Dobson, "Date and Composition," p. 183, note 1), is less secure than has been supposed. Talbot based the identification on what he called a "word for word" correspondence between "*P.*" and *AR*. In fact *P.* reads *regenerationis* and *remunerationis* for *AR crea-cionis* and *expectacionis* and continues as follows: *Conditor et redemptor corporis et anime. Esto mihi custos et medicus utriusque.* (Kennedy, p. 9) The divergent *Aves* may indicate that the author of *AR* had in mind a prayer other than *P.* Cf. two anonymous prayers markedly different from *P.* but with similar opening *Aves* (Wilmart, *Auteurs spirituels*, p. 23, note 2). The first, from MS Troyes 1900, fol. 110v (13th–14th century) reads as follows:

> *Ave principium nostre creationis. Ave precium nostre redemp-tionis. Ave viaticum nostre peregrinationis. Ave premium nostre remunerationis. Ave salvator mundi, rex glorie. Beatus venter qui te portavit et ubera quae succisti.*

The second, from Brit. Lib. MS Add. 16975, fol. 251v (Lire, Normandy; late 13th or beginning of 14th century) is identical in its first three lines to the above, but then continues as follows:

> *Ave partum* (sic) *nostre expectationis. Ave mundissima caro Christi, Domine Iesus Christe, fili Dei vivi, concede michi famulo tuo N. ut in finem vite mee sacratissimum corpus tuum vere possim agnoscere, fideliter adorare, salubriter per-cipere. Qui cum Deo Patre, etc.*

The *N.* in the sentence following the *Aves* above stands for *nomen* and indicates that the suppliant is to insert his name at that point in the prayer. There is no evidence that Wilmart's examples were composed by "*dominus P.*" or that they are derived from or even indirectly inspired by his prayer. Although they survive in comparatively late manuscripts, they and other such prayers seem likely to have circulated much earlier. Perhaps the author of *AR* had one such as these in mind. (R. D.)

9. *Tu esto nostrum gaudium.* Concluding passage, together with *Gloria tibi, Domine,* of hymns used for the vigil and feast of the Ascension. *Sar. B.,* 1: dcccclviii, dccccclxiii.

10. *Mane nobiscum, Domine.* Luke 24:29. Used as a versicle with the response *quoniam advesperascit* from the same passage, in vespers on a Sunday within the Easter octave. *Sar. B.,* 1:dcccclvii. These verses were known at Winchester as early as the eleventh century and somewhat later at Exeter. Talbot, p. 49, note 2; *AH,* 27:66. (R. D.)

11. *Gloria tibi, Domine.* Concluding passage in hymns honoring Our Lady, such as the hymn for matins on the Feast of the Annunciation. *Sar. B.,* 3:235. See note 9 above.

12. *Confiteor.* The confession of the Mass, beginning *Confiteor Deo omnipotenti,* was an early addition to the Divine Office, often being said in the course of or following prime. Tol., pp. 47–49.

13. *Adoramus te, Criste.* The first antiphon of matins on the feasts of the

Invention and the Exaltation of the Cross. *Sar. B.*, 3:276, 812. Also used as versicle and response in matins of the latter feast. *Sar. B.*, 3:818. Raw, who, when possible, cites liturgical texts from Anglo-Saxon times, finds this in *Port.*, 90:60, *Facs.*, p. 45, "Durham Ritual," p. 150, and elsewhere. Raw, pp. 264, note 36; 266, notes 55–6. On the five greetings, Cooper, pp. 12–14; also note 55 below. Raw (pp. 267–8) observes that in *AR* the number of prayers assigned is symbolically related to the intention of the prayers, as here, where five prayers are required in memory of the five wounds. (R. D.)

14. *Tuam crucem adoramus, Domine.* Response with *Adoramus te, Criste*; see note 13 above. *Sar. B.*, 3:814–15, 818–20. Also used as a Good Friday prayer to the cross. Gjerløw, pp. 27, 70. In addition, Raw (p. 264, note 37) cites *Port.*, 90:22, 60. *Tuam crucem* does not occur in "Durham Ritual," *contra* Raw, p. 267, note 57.

15. *Salue, crux sancta.* Hymn used as a sequence in the Mass of the Cross. Mone, 1:147; *Sar. B.*, 2:507; *AH*, 53:144; Raw, p. 264, note 38.

16. *Salue, crux que in corpore Cristi.* Antiphon in matins for the Feast of St. Andrew. *Sar. B.*, 3:20. Similar prayers are cited in Raw, p. 264, note 39.

17. *O Crux lignum triumphale . . . Sit in tuo nomine.* A variation of stanzas 18–19 of the hymn *Laudes crucis atollamus* (*AH*, 54:188–9), attributed to Adam of St. Victor (d. ca. 1192). Talbot, pp. 41–2; Raw p. 264, note 40. The Cleopatra and Corpus texts replace Adam's *Fit* with *Sit* in the last verse. More notably, in the sixth they adapt the hymn specifically for use by women by substituting feminine *sanas, egras* for Adam's masculine *sanos, egros*. Hymns addressed to the cross, much like those to the Virgin, repeat a number of phrases with slight variations. Some such phrases function also as versicles, responses, or antiphons. See Mone, 1:131–52. (R. D.)

18. *Miserere nostri, qui passus.* Conclusion of the antiphon *Tuam crucem adoramus.* See note 14 above.

19. *Vre Lauedi Vtsong.* Matins of the Office of Our Lady. See Tol., pp. 120–9, and *Prymer*, pp. 1 ff.

20. *falleð to þen eorðe.* Probably to kneel rather than to fall prostrate, although especially during Lent certain psalms were recited in a prone position. The customs in such matters are given in *The Use of Sarum*, 1:17, 22, 23, 66, 74, 97, etc.

21. *Domine, labia mea . . . Deus, in adiutorium . . . Gloria.* Pss. 50:17 and 69:2. Versicle, response, and "little doxology" which open the office following the private devotions. *Facs.*, 3, 19. *Deus, in adiutorium* is used at the beginning of the other hours except for compline, where it is preceded by *converte nos.* Tol., pp. 122–23.

22. *Venite.* Ps. 94. Used as an "invitatory" psalm in matins. *Facs.*, 19; *Sar. B.*, 1:xxxiii.

23. *Benedicite omnia.* Dan. 3:57. From the "canticle of the three children" assigned to Sunday Lauds of Our Lady and the canonical lauds as well.

*Facs.*, 6; *Sar. B.*, 2:31. The next to last verse, *Benedicamus patrem et filium*, is a Christian interpolation.

24. *Memento, salutis autor . . . Nascendo formam sumpseris.* Lines from a hymn *Christe redemptor omnium* used in Christmas matins, nocturns, third stanza. *Sar. B.*, 1:clxxi, *AH*, 2:36; 51:49.

25. *Te Deum . . . Non oruisti Virginis vterum.* A famous hymn sometimes ascribed to St. Nicetas (335–415). Raby, *Christian-Latin Poetry*, p. 106, note 2. Britt, pp. 14–20. The most common liturgical use has always been at the conclusion of matins. *Sar. B.*, 2:27–28.

26. *ex Maria Virgine.* From the Nicene or Mass Creed.

27. *Evch an segge hire vres as ha haueð iwriten ham.* As suggested in the Preface, this statement indicates that the original three anchoresses made their own copies of the Office of Our Lady, probably including the supplementary matter as well.

28. *Halirode Dai.* The Feast of the Exaltation of the Cross, 14 September. In the old monastic orders, the winter liturgical season began on this day, as noted in the General Introduction, p. 35.

29. *Preciosa.* Ps. 115:15. *Preciosa est in conspectu Domini, mors sanctorum eius,* a verse used as the beginning of the quasi-office of preciosa that came to be attached to prime. *Sar. B.*, 2:54.

30. *ani hichðe to speken.* Refraining from all conversation during certain periods was a general monastic practice. That such a rule of silence was imposed on communities of women is made clear in the customs of the Sisters of Syon. *The Myroure of Oure Ladye*, pp. xxxiii, 143, etc.

31. *Fidelium anime.* Versicle, which continues *per misericordiam Dei requiescant in pace.* Concludes prime and the little hour and also used after suffrages, as in the York litany. "York Breviary," 1:939. In the modern *Breviarium Romanum* this versicle comes at the conclusion of each hour except compline. Jungmann records its use in the close of the mass. 2:446, note 60.

32. *Placebo.* Ps. 114:9. Antiphon of the first psalm in Vespers of the Office of the Dead. *Placebo* thus came to designate the entire hour of vespers of that office just as *Dirige* (see note 34 below) referred to matins and lauds. For the Office of the Dead, see *Sar. B.*, 2:271–83, and 1:xlv–li. See also Tol., pp. 107–13.

33. *feste of niȝe leceons.* A reference to a feast day matins, which included three nocturns and therefore nine lessons. As indicated in the General Introduction, p. 34, Matins of the Office of Our Lady normally included no more than one nocturn, although three nocturns seem to be prescribed for days of commemoration "of ouwer front."

34. *Dirige.* Ps. 5:9. First antiphon in Matins of the Office of the Dead. *Sar. B.*, 2:273. See note 32 above.

35. *Requiem eternam.* Response in Vespers of the Office of the Dead and also of the Office of Our Lady. *Facs.*, 34.

36. *Magnificat*. Luke 1:46–55. Canticle occurring in Vespers of the Office of Our Lady. *Facs.*, 16, 33.

37. *Miserere*. Ps. 50. First psalm in Lauds of the Office of the Dead (*Sar. B.*, 2:281), also used in *memoriae* of the cross. *Facs.*, 46.

38. *Laudate*. Ps. 148. Last psalm in Lauds of the Office of the Dead (*Sar. B.*, 2:281), also used in the Lauds of the Office of Our Lady. *Facs.*, 6, 23, 34.

39. *Requiescant in pace*. Final phrase in the versicle *Fidelium anime*. See note 31 above. It was also used by itself, sometimes alternating with *Benedicamus Domino*. See note 40 below. *Sar. B.*, 2:283, and *The Use of Sarum*, 1:89.

40. *Benedicamus Domino*. Versicle used with *Deo gratias* near the close of the hours. See note 39 above. *Sar. B.*, 3:986.

41. *suffragies . . . commendaciun*. Suffrages are prayers intercessory in nature and may include prayers for the souls of the dead. Commendations are prayers for the dead at burials and commemorative services which usually end *Tibi, Domine, commendamus*. In religious houses, prayers for the souls of patrons were commonly recited on anniversaries. Tol., pp. 101–7, and *Prymer*, pp. 79 ff.

42. *Seoue Salmes*. The Seven Penitential Psalms, Nos. 6, 31, 37, 50, 101, 129, and 142, which were sung after prime and before the litany of the saints; Knowles, p. 715; Knowles, "Monastic Horarium," pp. 721–2. *Sar. B.*, 2:242–9; *Decreta Lanfranci*, pp. xxii, etc.; Tol., pp. 68–69; and *Prymer*, pp. 37 ff.

43. *letanie*. The litany of the saints, a set of prayers consisting of invocations, supplications, intercessions, and deprecations. In the monastic *horarium*, the litany generally followed prime, along with the Seven Penitential Psalms (see note 42 above). *Sar. B.*, 2:250–60; Tol., pp. 69–72; and *Prymer*, pp. 47 ff.

44. *Fiftene Salmes*. The Fifteen Gradual Psalms, Nos. 119–33. These psalms, each of which is entitled *canticum graduum*, or "song of ascents," in the Vulgate came to be a part of the monastic *cursus* and were usually inserted before matins as a private devotion. Tol., pp. 64–8; *Decreta Lanfranci*, pp. xxii, etc.; *Oxford Dictionary of the Christian Church*, s.v. Gradual Psalms; and *Prymer*, pp. 44 ff.

45. *Saluos fac seruos tuos*. Versicle and response used with the litany. *Sar. B.*, 2:254.

46. *Deus, cui proprium*. Prayer used with the litany and elsewhere, including the Office of the Dead. *Sar. B.*, 2:254, and *Prymer*, p. 50.

47. *Domine, fiat pax*. Ps. 121:7. Versicle used in several settings. See, for example, *Sar. B.*, 1:xi.

48. *Ecclesie tue quesumus, Domine*. Prayer used with the litany. *Here.*, 1:28.

49. *A porta inferi*. Versicle occurring in the Office of the Dead and elsewhere. *Sar. B.*, 2:281; and as antiphon *Here.*, 1:322.

50. *Fidelium*. A prayer found in the litany and elsewhere. "York

Breviary," 1:939, and *Here.*, 1:107, 2:42, 391. See note 75 below.

51. *Almichtin God.* This English prayer to the Trinity, associating God the Father with power, the Son with wisdom, and the Holy Spirit with love, may have been inspired by a Latin hymn similar to *In personis pluralitas*, which contains the passage *Summi patris potentia / Natique sapientia / Paracliti clementia. AH*, 34:44–45.

52. *Benedicamus Patrem et Filium.* Versicle used on Trinity in Lauds of Our Lady and elsewhere. *Facs.*, 25, and *Sar. B.*, 1:mxlviii.

53. *Omnipotens sempiterne Deus.* A well-known prayer used in such settings as Vespers of the Feast of the Trinity, Lauds of Our Lady, and as the Mass collect on Trinity Sunday. Raw, p. 262, note 22. As a collect, it is still prescribed in the Roman Missal as well as *The Book of Common Prayer. Sar. B.*, 1:mxlvii; *Facs.*, 10; *The Sarum Missal*, p. 170; "Durham Ritual," p. 158; Massey H. Shepherd, p. 186.

54. *Alpha et omega.* The phrase, from Apoc. 1:8, opens a hymn to the Trinity by Hildebert of Lavardin (1056–1133). *AH*, 50:409–11; Szöverffy, 2:37–9. In Raby's view the hymn, which may have been composed during Hildebert's exile in England, "ranks as one of the few masterpieces of the mystical verse of the Middle Ages" (*Christian-Latin Poetry*, pp. 269–70). (R. D.)

55. *Iesu þin are.* The "pentad" of the five wounds was well established in literature, art, and interpretations of the liturgy. See, for example, the discussion of Goscelin's *Liber Confortorius* in the General Introduction, p. 12. Also, note the references in thirteenth-century lyrics. Brown, *English Lyrics*, pp. 6:102; 66:24. St. Bernard of Clairvaux (d. 1153) is particularly associated with the spread of special devotion to the five wounds. *New Catholic Encyclopedia*, 14:1036. Also, Raw, p. 271, note 54. (R. D.)

56. *Omnis terra adoret.* Versicle used in *memoriae* of the cross in matins. *Sar. B.*, 2:92.

57. *Iuste iudex.* Probably the hymn by Berengar of Tours (999–1088). So Raw (p. 265, note 47) and Salu (p. 11). The full text is given in Mone, 1:359. On Berengar see Raby, *Christian-Latin Poetry*, pp. 263–4. Another hymn, however, used in none on the Feast of the Nativity, begins with the same phrase. *Here.*, 1:21. (R. D.)

58. *seoue ʒeouen of þe Hali Gast.* The seven gifts in Isaiah 11:2. See the enumeration of the gifts by St. Thomas Aquinas, *Summa Theologica*, I-II, q. 68, art. 4, Vol. 1:880–81. The seven gifts were often associated with other "heptads" like the seven virtues in popular religious treatises, such as the *Ayenbite of Inwyt*, pp. 118–19 and passim.

59. *seoue tiden.* The seven hours of the Divine Office. See the General Introduction, pp. 29–38.

60. *seoue bonen in þe Pater Noster.* The seven "petitions" in terms of which the *Pater Noster* was commonly expounded in doctrinal treatises. *Ayenbite of Inwyt*, pp. 99–118, and *The Myroure of Oure Ladye*, pp. 73–7.

61. *seouen heaued ant dedliche sunnen.* The seven capital sins: pride, avarice,

lechery, wrath, gluttony, envy, and sloth. For a classical commentary, see St. Thomas, I-II, q. 84, art. 4, Vol. 1:964–65. The authors of doctrinal treatises include vivid portrayals of the sins and their branches. See, for example, *Ayenbite of Inwyt*, pp. 14–70.

62. *seouene seli eadinessen*. Matt. 5:3 ff. The beatitudes are generally considered in modern times to be eight in number, but in the Middle Ages they were variously enumerated. See St. Thomas, II, q. 69, art. 3, Vol. 2:887–89.

63. *Deus, cui omne cor patet*. A very well-known collect "for purity" dating at least from the time of Alcuin. It was used in various liturgical settings in the Sarum and Roman Uses and appears in Lauds of Our Lady. *Facs.*, 25; *Sar. B.*, 2:481; Massey H. Shepherd, p. 67.

64. *Exaudi quesumus, Domine*. Prayer used in the litany and elsewhere. *Facs.*, 41, and *Decreta Lanfranci*, p. 18.

65. *Ego dixi, Domine*. Response in matins for the week following the octave of Epiphany, and elsewhere. *Here.*, 1:222; *New Min.*, p. 23.

66. *þe tweolf boȝes þe bloweð of cherite*. The reference is to the well-known allegory of the tree of charity with twelve blossoming branches, based on 1 Cor. 13:4–7. Used as the *capitulum* in sext for the week following Quinquagesima. *Sar. B.*, 1:dlii.

67. *Annunciaverunt opera Dei*. Versicle, with response *Et facta eius intellexerunt*, used in lauds on feasts of the Apostles. *Sar. B.*, 2:369, and *Here.*, 2:211.

68. *Exaudi nos, Deus*. Collect used on feasts of the Apostles. *Here.*, 1:42.

69. *þe six werkes of milce*. Matt. 25:35–36. To the original six works of bodily mercy — visiting the ill, giving drink to the thirsty, giving food to the hungry, ransoming the prisoner, covering the naked, and harboring the homeless — a seventh, burying the dead, came to be added. These seven works were incorporated in doctrinal treatises. *Speculum Christiani*, pp. 40–44.

70. *Dispersit, dedit*. Versicle used before lauds. *Sar. B.*, 3:655.

71. *Retribuere dignari*. Prayer used after dinner. *The Use of Sarum*, 1:245. Also a prayer commonly said for benefactors. Cooper, p. 33.

72. *þe fouwer marheȝeuen*. The four "dotes" or qualities of the resurrected body, based on 1 Cor. 15:42–44. The author of *AR* refers to the "wedding gifts" of souls in heaven. See St. Thomas, supp., q. 82, art. 1; q. 83, art. 1; q. 84, art. 1; q. 85, art. 1, Vol. 3:2904–25.

73. *nihene englene weoredes*. The more or less standard nine orders: angels, archangels, virtues, powers, principalities, dominations, thrones, cherubim, and seraphim. See St. Thomas, I, q. 108, art. 6, Vol. 1:528–35.

74. *De profundis*. Ps. 129. Used in Vespers of Our Lady and elsewhere. *Facs.*, 34, 47.

75. *Fidelium*. MS Cotton Nero A.XIV, ed. Day, p. 13, provides an expanded reading at this point — *Fidelium, Deus, omnium conditor et redemptor, animabus famulorum famularumque*. This prayer is found in the litany and

elsewhere. See note 50 above. A prayer with the same wording as far as *animabus* but continuing *omnium fidelium defunctorum* is found in the litany in *Sar. B.* 2:255.

76. A similar concern for Christians in heathendom is expressed in Innocent III's encyclical of 1213, *De negotio terrae sanctae* (Dobson, *Origins of Ancrene Wisse*, pp. 239-40). (R. D.)
*Leuaui oculos meos.* Ps. 120. Used in prime and vespers. *Sar. B.*, 2:56, 198.

77. *Conuertere, Domine. Usquequo.* Prayer used on Ash Wednesday and also for the blessing of weapons. *Manuale ad Usum Percelebris Ecclesie Sarisburiensis*, pp. 10, 16, 68.

78. *Pretende, Domine.* Collect used in the litany. *Here.*, 1:28.

79. *Ecce, salus mundi.* Invocation used at the consecration, like *Aue, principium nostre creacionis* (see note 8 above). The initial word is usually *ave* or *salve* rather than *ecce*. Jungmann, 2:215.

80. See notes 8 and 9 above.

81. *Sed quis est locus.* Based on St. Augustine, *Confessions*, I, Chaps. 2, 5. Cooper, pp. 36-37.

82. See note 37 above.

83. *Concede quesumus.* Prayer in Lauds of Our Lady. *Facs.* 24.

84. *Messe-cos.* The *pax domini* of the Mass. Jungmann, 2:321 ff.

85. *iwrite þruppe.* Fols. 9v-10r and notes 13-17 above. The five greetings (*Adoramus te* through *O crux lignum*) here initiate a set to be repeated five times, except that each repetition requires a different psalm and concluding orison, as specified below in the text. (R. D.)

86. *Salua nos, Criste.* Antiphon used on the Feast of the Exaltation of the Cross. *Here.*, 2:327. Raw (pp. 264, note 41; 267, note 58) cites further *Port.* 90:22, 24; Cotton MSS Tiberius A. III, Titus D. XXVII. See note 88 below.

87. *Iubilate.* Ps. 99. Used in Lauds of Our Lady. *Facs.*, 6, 22.

88. *Qui saluasti Petrum in mari.* Based on Matt. 14:28-31. Continuation of the antiphon *Salua nos, Criste* used in *memoriae* of Our Lady. *Sar. B.*, 2:94.

89. *Protector noster.* Ps. 83:10. Used in matins. *Sar. B.*, 2:152. Raw (p. 264, note 42) cites further "Durham Ritual," p. 15.

90. *Deus, qui sanctam crucem.* Collect or antiphon used at matins in *memoriae* of the cross. *Here.*, 2:14; *Sar. B.*, 2:92.

91. *Adesto quesumus, Domine, Deus noster, et quos sancte crucis.* A variant, from which *quesumus* is omitted, occurs as a post-communion prayer after the Mass of the Holy Cross in *The Sarum Missal*, p. 387. Raw (pp. 264-5, 267, notes 44, 59) cites further "Durham Ritual," p. 94 (with *ut* in place of *et*) and p. 150.

92. *Qui confidunt.* Ps. 124. Used in vespers. *Sar. B.*, 2:200.

93. *Domine, non est exaltatum.* Ps. 130. Used in vespers. *Sar. B.*, 2:204.

94. *Laudate Dominum in sanctis eius.* Ps. 150:1. Used in lauds. *Sar. B.*, 2:33.

95. See note 90 above.

96. *Adesto.* See note 91 above.

97. *Deus, qui pro nobis Filium.* Collect at the baptismal font in vespers on Easter and elsewhere. *Sar. B.*, 1:dcccxxi, dcccxxix. Raw, p. 265.

98. *Deus, qui vnigeniti Filii tui.* Mass prayer on the Feast of the Exaltation of the Cross. *The Sarum Missal*, p. 320. A somewhat different form occurs in the Mass of the Cross. *The Sarum Missal*, p. 386. Raw (p. 264, note 46) finds occurrences in *Port.*, 89:108; *New Min.*, p. 212; *The Leofric Missal*, p. 178; MS Cotton Titus D. XXVI, fol. 56v; and "Durham Ritual," p. 94. (R. D.)

99. *Iuste Iudex.* See note 57 above. This is the last of the orisons in the series (note 85 above).

100. *O beata et intemerata.* Variant of a prayer to the Virgin and St. John. The same form occurs in Brit. Lib. MS Royal 2A XXII, fol. 201, a Westminster Abbey psalter. Wilmart, *Auteurs spirituels*, pp. 474-504, esp. 487-8, variant of line 3. This prayer evidently is intended as a coda to the series just completed. (R. D.)

101. *Leauedi Seinte Marie.* The five English prayers beginning with this phrase celebrate the five joys of Our Lady — the Annunciation, the Nativity, the Resurrection, the Ascension, and the Assumption — and may well have been inspired by Latin hymns similar to those underlying certain Middle English lyrics. See Brown, *Religious Lyrics*, pp. 18, 248. The theme of five joys was especially popular in England in contrast to the seven joys figuring in works originating on the Continent. Later, fifteen and even twenty-five joys were distinguished. Wilmart, *Auteurs spirituels*, pp. 326-36, and *The Poems of John of Hoveden*, pp. xxvii ff. See also *The Poems of William of Shoreham*, pp. 115-26. See also Talbot, pp. 42 ff. Included in this series are five Latin prayers whose initial letters spell MARIA. See note 120 below.

102. *Ad Dominum cum tribularer.* Ps. 119. The first of the Fifteen Gradual Psalms. See note 44 above.

103. *Retribue.* Ps. 118:17. Used in prime and elsewhere. *Facs.*, 8, 27, *Sar.B.*, 2:45.

104. *In conuertendo.* Ps. 125. Another of the Fifteen Gradual Psalms. See note 44 above. *Sar. B.*, 1:xxxviii.

105. *Ad te leuaui.* Ps. 122. Another of the Fifteen Gradual Psalms. See note 44 above. In lauds, *Sar. B.*, 2:36.

106. *Spiritus Sanctus superveniet in te.* Luke 1:35. Versicle used on the Feast of the Annunciation. *The Sarum Missal*, p. 259. Raw (p. 261, note 6) cites *New Min.*, p. 84. This versicle is the first in a series of five, each followed by a collect, and each collect but the last (*O sancta Virgo uirginum*) followed by an antiphon. (R. D.)

107. *Gratiam tuam.* Collect used in Easter Vespers of Our Lady. *Here.*, 1:331; 3:6. Raw (p. 261, note 7) cites *New Min.*, p. 84, and *Port.*, 89:99.

108. *Aue, Regina celorum.* Antiphon used on the Feast of the Nativity of Our Lady. *Sar.B.*, 3:784. Raw, p. 261, note 8. Authorship unknown. Britt, p. 66, dates it ante 1300. (R. D.)

109. *Egredietur uirga de radice Iesse.* Isaiah 11:1. Versicle and response used in *memoriae* of Our Lady and elsewhere. *Sar. B.*, 1:xxxii ff., 3:238. Raw (p. 261, note 9) finds this form also used in Chapter for vespers of the second Sunday in Advent, in *Port.*, 89:2.

110. *Deus, qui virginalem aulam.* Collect used in matins on the Feast of the Assumption. *Sar. B.*, 3:687. Raw (p. 261, note 10) cites *New Min.*, p. 144, and *Port.*, 89:105; also "Durham Ritual," p. 66.

111. *Gaude, Dei genitrix, Virgo immaculata.* Antiphon used in Terce of Our Lady and elsewhere. *Facs.*, 29, 56. Raw, p. 261, note 11; Wilmart, *Auteurs spirituels*, pp. 331-6. (R. D.)

112. *Ecce, in utero concipies.* Luke 1:31. Versicle used in Matins of the Annunciation. Raw (p. 261, note 15) cites *Sar. B.*, 3:238. In the Corpus and Vitellius MSS this versicle is the fourth rather than the third in the sequence. See note 115 below. (R. D.)

113. *Deus, qui de beate Marie semper.* Cleopatra differs from MSS Corpus and Cotton Vitellius F. VII, which have *Deus, qui de beate Marie uirginis utero*, a collect used in Matins of Our Lady and elsewhere. Some of the following texts deviate slightly from the wording of *AR. Facs.*, 6; *Here.*, 1:111; 2:26, 131; *Sar. B.*, 2:289. Raw (p. 261, note 13) cites further *New Min.*, p. 83; *Port.*, 89:98; *The Leofric Missal*, p. 71; and the "Durham Ritual," p. 51. (R. D.)

114. *Gaude, Virgo . . . ante Dominum.* Evidently an antiphon in keeping with the pattern of preceding meditations on Our Lady (see note 106 above). As such, the form is untraced, as stated by Raw (p. 261, note 14), Cooper (p. 45), and Magee (p. 84). It may be worth noting, however, that *Gaude, Virgo* is a common opening for antiphons specified for the feasts of the Annunciation, Conception, and Purification. *Sar. B.*, 1: xxxiv, etc. The phrase *Gaudeat ecclesia* begins a large number of hymns. *AH*, 5:126, 219; 7:70; 8:86, etc.

115. *Ecce, Virgo concipiet.* Isaiah 7:14. Used with some alterations as a *capitulum* on Advent in Lauds of Our Lady and elsewhere. *Sar. B.*, 1:xxxvi, 3:233, and *Here.*, 2:133. Raw (p. 261, note 12) refers to other occurrences in *Port.*, 89:2, 98, and *New Min.*, p. 84. In the Corpus and Vitellius MSS this versicle is the third in the sequence. See note 112 above. (R. D.)

116. *Deus, qui salutis.* Collect used in Terce and Vespers of Our Lady. *Facs.*, 16, 29; *The Leofric Missal*, p. 65. Raw, p. 261, note 16. Also, *Here.*, 1:151; 2:11, 31; *Sar. B.*, 1:191. (R. D.)

117. *Alma Redemptoris Mater.* *AH*, 50:317. The hymn dates from the eleventh century. Ascription of authorship to Herimannus Contractus (Hermann of Reichenau, 1013-54) is disputed. Britt, p. 65; Raby, *Christian-Latin Poetry*, p. 227; Szövérffy, 1:376-7. This hymn is used as an antiphon for the Nativity of the Virgin. Raw (p. 262, note 17) cites *Sar. B.*, 3:784. In addition, *Here.*, 2:34, note a. For Trinity, *Here.* 3:74. For the octave of the Assumption, "York Breviary," 2:494. (R. D.)

118. *Ecce, ancilla Domini*. Luke 1:38. Antiphon used on the Feast of the Annunciation. "York Breviary," 2:234.

119. *O sancta Virgo uirginum*. MS Cotton Nero A. XIV, ed. Day, p. 18, provides an expanded reading:

> *O sancta Uirgo uirginum, Que genuisti filium, Trium-*
> *phatorem zabuli.* (O holy Virgin of virgins, Who gave
> birth to a son, Vanquisher of the devil.)

The first three verses of the *Oratio ad Sanctam Mariam* by Marbod of Rennes (ca. 1035–1123), except that Nero has *filium* for Marbod's *Dominum*. *AH*, 50:395; Raw, p. 262, note 19. An account of Marbod, whose poetry was highly esteemed by contemporaries such as Hildebert (note 54 above), appears in Raby, *Christian-Latin Poetry*, pp. 273–7. This collect concludes the series begun with *Spiritus Sanctus* (note 106 above). (R. D.)

120. *þe fif letteres of Vre Lauedi nome*. The series begins at the bottom of fol. 15v: *Magnificat* (a canticle from Luke 1:46–55 rather than a psalm), *Ad Dominum cum tribularer* (Ps. 119:1), *Retribue servo tuo* (Ps. 118:17), *In conuertendo* (Ps. 125:1), and *Ad te leuaui* (Ps. 122:1). Devotion dated between 1184 and 1203; Talbot, pp. 42–3.

121. The meaning of the sentence is obscure.

122. *þe vres of þe Hali Gast*. The Office of the Holy Ghost. This office is of infrequent occurrence in available medieval service books as compared with the Office of the Dead, for example. In his discussion of the Office of the Holy Ghost, Talbot, pp. 43–46, refers to its appearance in a book of hours preserved in MS Egerton 1151, of the early thirteenth century. Conceivably, the office as given therein approximates that which the anchoresses were to recite on an optional basis.

123. *Benedicite; potum nostrum*. Monastic blessing at table. *Decreta Lanfranci*, pp. 30, 32, and *The Use of Sarum*, pp. 242 ff.

124. *Adiutorium nostrum*. Versicle, frequently followed by the *Gloria*, used in the capitular office and elsewhere. Tol., p. 53, and *Here.*, 1:345; as antiphon, *Here.* 3:22.

125. *Uisita, Domine, habitationem istam*. Prayer used at the end of Compline of Our Lady. *Facs.*, 18.

126. *Cristus vincit*. Antiphon used at Easter. For a similar formulation, see *AH*, 15:50–51. Cooper (p. 52) states that this antiphon was used as part of the acclamations or *laudes* sung at coronations from the time of Charlemagne.

127. *Ecce crucem Domini*. Antiphon used in lauds and elsewhere on the Feast of the Exaltation of the Cross. *Sar. B.*, 3:823, 824.

128. See fol. 10v and note 21 above.

129. *Crux fugat omne malum*. Although this hymn seems not to occur in the standard collections, several similar hymns are to be found. Thus, a short poem ascribed to Reinerus, a monk of the twelfth century, begins *Crux vitae signum domat et fugat omne malignum*. *PL*, 204:97–98. We are indebted to Professor George H. Brown of Stanford University for calling

this poem to our attention. Again, the following passage appears in a somewhat later hymn: *Crux excellit omne donum / Et acquirit omne bonum / Suis amatoribus. / Crux expellit omne metum / Et cor facit esse laetum / Plenumque fulgoribus. AH,* 50:575.

# Bibliography and Abbreviations

Publications referred to in the notes to the General Introduction and to the text of the Introduction and Part I of *AR* are indicated by author, editor, or short title, as shown in the Bibliography. Abbreviations, given in brackets below at the end of appropriate entries, are used for frequently cited works.

Ackerman, Robert W. "*The Debate of the Body and the Soul* and Parochial Christianity." *Speculum*, 37 (1962):541–65.

Ackerman, Robert W. "The Liturgical Day in *Ancrene Riwle*." *Speculum*, 53 (1978):734–44.

Ailred, St. "The 'De Institutis Inclusarum' of Ailred of Rievaulx." Edited by C. H. Talbot, *Analecta Sacri Ordinis Cisterciensis*, 7 (1951): Fasc. 3–4, 167–217.

Allen, Hope Emily. "Wynkyn de Worde and a Second French Compilation from the 'Ancren Riwle,' with a Description of the First." In *Essays and Studies in Honor of Carleton Brown*, pp. 182–219. New York: New York University Press, 1940.

*Analecta Hymnica Medii Aevi*. Edited by C. Blume and G. M. Dreves. 55 vols. Leipzig: O. R. Reisland, 1886–1922.                    [*AH*]

*An Anglo-Saxon Dictionary*. Edited by Joseph Bosworth. Revised by T. Northcote Toller. Oxford: Oxford University Press, 1898.

Augustine, St. *St. Augustine's Confessions, with an English Translation by William Watts*. Loeb Classical Library. London: Heinemann, 1931.

*Ayenbite of Inwyt, Dan Michel's*. Edited by Richard Morris. EETS, 23 (1866).

Baldwin, Mary. "Some Difficult Words in the *Ancrene Riwle*." *Mediaeval Studies*, 38 (1976):268–90, especially 272–77.

Batiffol, Pierre. *History of the Roman Breviary*. Translated by Atwell

M. Y. Baylay. London: Longmans Green, 1912.

Baugh, Albert C., ed. *A Literary History of England.* 2nd ed. Vol. I: *The Middle Ages,* by Kemp Malone and Albert C. Baugh. New York: Appleton-Century-Crofts, 1967.

*Benedicti Regula.* Edited by Rudolph Hanslik. Corpus Scriptorum Ecclesiasticorum Latinorum, 75. Vienna: Hoelder-Pichler-Tempsky, 1960.

Bishop, Edmund. *Liturgica Historica: Papers on the Liturgy and Religious Life of the Western Church.* Oxford: Clarendon Press, 1918.

Bramlette, E. E. "The Original Language of the *Ancren Riwle.*" *Anglia,* 15 (1893):478–98.

Britt, Matthew, ed. *The Hymns of the Breviary and Missal.* New York: Benziger, 1955.

Brown, Carleton, ed. *English Lyrics of the XIIIth Century.* Oxford: Clarendon Press, 1932.

Brown, Carleton, ed. *Religious Lyrics of the XIVth Century.* 2nd edition. Revised by G. V. Smithers. Oxford: Clarendon Press, 1952.

*Butler's Lives of the Saints.* Revised by Herbert Thurston and Donald Attwater. 4 vols. Westminster: Palm, 1956.

*Cambridge History of English Literature, The.* Edited by A. W. Ward and A. R. Waller. 15 vols. Cambridge: University Press, 1933.

Chambers, R. W. *On the Continuity of English Prose from Alfred to More and His School.* From the Introduction to *Nicholas Harpsfield's Life of Sir Thomas More.* EETS, 186 (1932). Repr. EETS, 191 A (1957).

Chambers, R. W. "Recent Research upon the *Ancren Riwle.*" *Review of English Studies,* 1 (1925):4–23.

Clay, Rotha M. *The Hermits and Anchorites of England.* London: SPCK, 1914.

*Codex Iuris Canonici Pii X.* Edited by Pietro Card. Gasparri. Westminster, Md.: Newman Press, 1957.

*Consuetudines Beccenses.* Edited by Marie Pascal Dickson. Corpus Consuetudinum Monasticarum, 4. Siegburg: F. Schmitt, 1967.

Cook, G. H. *The English Mediaeval Parish Church.* London: Phoenix House, 1954.

Cooper, Josephine G. (Ethelbert), Sister. "Latin Elements of the 'Ancrene Riwle.'" Ph.D. dissertation, University of Birmingham, 1956.

Dahood, Roger. "A Lexical Puzzle in 'Ancrene Wisse.'" *Notes and Queries,* ns 25 (1978):1–2, 541.

Darwin, Francis D. S. *The English Mediaeval Recluse*. London: SPCK, [1944].

Day, Mabel, ed. *The English Text of the Ancrene Riwle, Cotton Nero A.XIV*. EETS, 225 (1952).

*Decreta Lanfranci Monachis Cantuariensibus Transmissa*. Edited by David Knowles. Corpus Consuetudinum Monasticarum, 3 (1967).

Delatte, Paul. *Commentary on the Rule of St. Benedict*, translated by Justin McCann. London: Burns, Oates, and Washburn, 1921.

Dix, Gregory. *The Shape of the Liturgy*. 2nd ed. Westminster: Dacre Press, 1954.

Dobson, E. J. "The Affiliations of the Manuscripts of *Ancrene Wisse*." In *English and Medieval Studies Presented to J. R. R. Tolkien on the Occasion of his Seventieth Birthday*. Edited by Norman Davis and C. L. Wrenn, pp. 128–63. London: Allen and Unwin, 1962.

Dobson, E. J. "The Date and Composition of Ancrene Wisse." In *Proceedings of the British Academy* 52:181–208. London: Oxford University Press, 1966.

Dobson, E. J., ed. *The English Text of the Ancrene Riwle, B. M. Cotton MS Cleopatra C. VI*. EETS, 267 (1972).      [Dobs.]

Dobson, E. J. *The Origins of Ancrene Wisse*. Oxford: Clarendon Press, 1976.

Doob, Penelope B. R. *Nebuchadnezzar's Children: Conventions of Madness in Middle English Literature*. New Haven: Yale University Press, 1974.

"Durham Ritual." *Rituale Ecclesiae Dunelmensis*. Edited by U. Lindelöf. Surtees Society, 140 (1927).

Dymes, Dorothy. "The Original Language of *Ancren Riwle*." In *Essays and Studies by Members of the English Association*, 9 (1924): 31–49.

Early English Text Society.      [EETS]

*Facsimiles of Horae de Beata Maria Virgine from English MSS. of the Eleventh Century*. Edited by E. S. Dewick. Henry Bradshaw Society, 21 (1902).      [*Facs.*]

Felperin, Winnifred M. "The Art of Perfection: A Study in the Imagery and Instruction of the *Ancrene Riwle*." Ph.D. dissertation, Harvard University, 1966.

Gjerløw, Lilli. *Adoratio Crucis: The Regularis Concordia and the Decreta Lanfranci*. Oslo: Norwegian Universities Press, 1961.

Gougaud, Louis. *Dévotions et pratiques ascétiques du moyen âge*. Paris: Abbaye de Maredsous, 1925.

Gougaud, Louis. *Ermites et réclus: Etudes sur d'anciennes formes de vie religieuse*. Paris: Abbaye Saint-Martin de Ligugé, 1928.

Gray, John Hubert. "The Influence of Confessional Literature on the Composition of the *Ancrene Riwle*." Ph.D. dissertation, London University, 1961.

Grayson, Janet. *Structure and Imagery in "Ancrene Wisse."* Hanover, NH: University Press of New England, 1974.

Grimlaic. *Regula Solitariorum*. Patrologia Latina, 103:573–664.

Hastings, George S. "Two Aspects of Style in the AB Dialect of Middle English." Ph.D. dissertation, University of Pennsylvania, 1965.

Herbert, J. A., ed. *The French Text of the Ancrene Riwle, British Museum MS. Cotton Vitellius F.VII*. EETS, 219 (1944, repr. 1967).

*The Hereford Breviary*. Edited by Walter Howard Frere and Langton E. G. Brown. Henry Bradshaw Society, 26, 40, 46 (1904, 1911, 1915). [*Here.*]

Hickes, George. *Linguarum veterum Septentrionalium Thesaurus Grammatico-Criticus et Archaeologicus*. 2 vols. Oxford: Sheldonian Theatre, 1703, 1705.

*John of Hoveden, Poems of*. Edited by F. J. E. Raby. Surtees Society, 154 (1939).

Jungmann, Josef A. *The Mass of the Roman Rite: Its Origins and Development*. Translated by Francis A. Brunner. 2 vols. New York: Benziger, 1955.

Käsmann, Hans. "Zur Frage der ursprünglichen Fassung der *Ancrene Riwle*." *Anglia*, 75 (1957):134–56.

Kennedy, V. L. "The Handbook of Master Peter Chancellor of Chartres," *Mediaeval Studies*, 5 (1943):1–38.

Knowles, David. "The Monastic Horarium, 970–1120." *Downside Review*, 51 (1933):706–25.

Knowles, David. *The Monastic Order in England from the Times of St. Dunstan to the Fourth Lateran Council, 940–1216*. Cambridge: University Press, 2nd ed., reprinted 1966. [Knowles]

Leclercq, Jean. "Études sur le vocabulaire monastique du moyen âge." *Studia Anselmiana*, 48. Rome: Herder, 1961.

*Leofric Missal, The, as Used in the Cathedral of Exeter during the Episcopate of its First Bishop, A.D. 1050–1072*. Edited by F. E. Warren. Oxford: Clarendon Press, 1883.

Macaulay, G. C. " 'Ancren Riwle.' " *Modern Language Review*, 9 (1914):63–78, 145–70, 324–31, 462–74.

MacKean, W. H. *Christian Monasticism in Egypt to the Close of the Fourth Century*. London: SPCK, 1920.

Madden, Sir Frederic. "The 'Ancren Riwle.' " *Notes & Queries*, 9 (1854):5–6.

Madden, Sir Frederic. Unpublished diary. Bodley MS hist. C. 140–82.

Magee, Glenys. "The *Ancrene Wisse*: Part I." Master's thesis, University of Keele, 1969.

Magoun, Francis P., Jr. "*Ancrene Wisse* vs. *Ancren Riwle*." *English Literary History*, 4 (1937):112–13.

*Manuale ad Usum percelebris Ecclesie Sarisburiensis*. Edited by A. Jeffries Collins. Henry Bradshaw Society, 91 (1960).

*Middle English Dictionary*. Edited by Hans Kurath and Sherman Kuhn. Ann Arbor, Mich.: University of Michigan Press, 1952–. [*MED*]

Mone, Franz Joseph, ed. *Lateinische Hymnen des Mittelalters*. 3 vols. 1853–55. Reprint Aalen: Scientia, 1964.

Montalembert, Count Charles de. *The Monks of the West from St. Benedict to St. Bernard*. 6 vols. Authorized translation. London: John C. Nimmo, 1896.

Moorman, John R. H. *Church Life in England in the Thirteenth Century*. Cambridge: University Press, reprinted 1955.

Morton, James, ed. *The Ancren Riwle: A Treatise on the Rules and Duties of Monastic Life*. Camden Society, 57 (1853).

*Myroure of Oure Ladye, The*. Edited by John Henry Blunt. EETS, es, 19 (1873).

New Catholic Encyclopedia. 16 vols. New York: McGraw-Hill, 1967.

*New Minster, Winchester, The Missal of the*. Edited by D. H. Turner. Henry Bradshaw Society, 93 (1962). [*New Min.*]

O'Leary, De Lacy. *The Saints of Egypt*. London: SPCK, 1937.

Oliger, Paul Livarius. "Regulae tres Reclusorum et Eremitarum Angliae saec. XIII–XIV." *Antonianum*, 3 (1928):151–190, 299–320.

*Oxford Dictionary of the Christian Church, The*. Edited by F. L. Cross and E. A. Livingstone. 2nd ed. London: Oxford University Press, 1974.

*Oxford English Dictionary, The*. Edited by James A. H. Murray, *et al.* 13 vols. Oxford: Clarendon Press, 1933. [*OED*]

"Patrologia Latina." *Patrologiae Cursus Completus*: Series Latina. Paris: Garnier, 1844–65. Edited by J.-P. Migne.

*Portiforium of Saint Wulfstan, The*. Edited by Anselm Hughes. Henry

Bradshaw Society, 89, 90 (1958, 1960). *[Port.]*

Powicke, F. M., tr. *The Life of Ailred of Rievaulx by Walter Daniel.* London: Nelson, 1950.

*Prymer or Lay Folks' Prayer Book, The.* Edited by Henry Littlehales, with an introduction by Edmund Bishop. EETS, 105, 109 (1895-1897).

Raby, F. J. E. *A History of Christian-Latin Poetry from the Beginnings to the Close of the Middle Ages.* Oxford: Clarendon Press, 1927.

Raw, Barbara, "The Prayers and Devotions in the *Ancrene Wisse.*" In *Chaucer and Middle English Studies in Honour of Rossell Hope Robbins.* Edited by Beryl Rowland, pp. 260-71. London: George Allen and Unwin, 1974.

*Regularis Concordia Anglicae Nationis Monachorum Sanctimonialiumque.* Edited and translated by Thomas Symons. London: Thomas Nelson and Sons, 1953. *[Reg. Con.]*

Russell, Josiah Cox. "The Clerical Population of Medieval England." *Traditio,* 2 (1944):177-212.

Salmon, Pierre. *The Breviary through the Centuries.* Translated by Sister David Mary, S.N.J.M. Collegeville, Minn.: Liturgical Press, 1962.

Salu, Mary B., tr. *The Ancrene Riwle (The Corpus MS: Ancrene Wisse).* Notre Dame, Ind.: University of Notre Dame Press, 1956.

Samuels, M. L. "*Ancrene Riwle* Studies," *Medium Ævum,* 22 (1953):1-9.

"Sarum Breviary." *Breviarium ad Usum Insignis Ecclesiae Sarum.* 3 vols. Edited by Francis Procter and Christopher Wordsworth, Cambridge: University Press, 1882, 1879, 1886. *[Sar. B.]*

*Sarum Missal Edited from Three Early Manuscripts, The.* Edited by J. Wickham Legg. Oxford University Press, 1916, reprinted 1969.

Schofield, William H. *English Literature from the Norman Conquest to Chaucer.* New York: Macmillan, 1906.

Severs, J. Burke, ed. *A Manual of the Writings in Middle English, 1050-1500.* Vol. 2. New Haven, Conn.: Connecticut Academy of Arts and Sciences, 1970.

Shepherd, Geoffrey, ed. *Ancrene Wisse, Parts Six and Seven.* London: Nelson, 1959.

Shepherd, Massey Hamilton, Jr. *The Oxford American Prayer Book Commentary.* New York: Oxford University Press, 1950.

*Speculum Christiani.* Edited by Gustav Holmstedt. EETS, 182 (1933).

Steele, Francesca M. *Anchoresses of the West*. St. Louis, Mo.: Herder, 1903.

Szövérffy, Josef. *Die Annalen der lateinischen Hymnendichtung: Ein Handbuch*. 2 vols. Berlin: Erich Schmidt, 1964-1965.

Talbot, C. H. "Some Notes on the Dating of the *Ancrene Riwle*." *Neophilologus*, 40 (1956):38-50.

Thomas Aquinas, St. *Summa Theologica, Literally Translated by the Fathers of the English Dominican Province*. 3 vols. New York: Benziger, 1947-1948.

Tolhurst, J. B. L. "Introduction to the English Monastic Breviaries." *The Monastic Breviary of Hyde Abbey, Winchester*. Vol. 6. Edited by J. B. L. Tolhurst. Henry Bradshaw Society, 80 (1942). [*Tol.*]

Tolkien, J. R. R., ed. *The English Text of the Ancrene Riwle: Ancrene Wisse, MS Corpus Christi College Cambridge 402*. EETS, 249 (1962).

*Use of Sarum, The: The Sarum Customs as Set Forth in the Consuetudinary and Customary*. Edited by Walter Howard Frere. Cambridge: University Press, 1898, reprinted edition, 1969.

*Vices and Virtues*. Edited by F. Holthausen. Pt. I. EETS, 89 (1888).

Waddell, Helen, tr. *The Desert Fathers*. Ann Arbor, Mich.: University of Michigan Press, 1957.

"Westminster Missal." *Missale ad Usum Ecclesie Westmonasteriensis*. Edited by J. Wickham Legg. 3 vols. Henry Bradshaw Society, 1, 5, 12 (1891, 1893, 1897).

*William of Shoreham, The Poems of*. Edited by M. Konrath, EETS, es, 86 (1902).

Williams, George H. *Wilderness and Paradise in Christian Thought*. New York: Harper, 1962.

Wilmart, André. *Auteurs spirituels et dévots du moyen âge latin*. Paris: Librairie Bloud et Gay, 1932.

Wilmart, André. "Ève et Goscelin." *Revue Bénédictine*, 50 (1938):42-83.

Wilmart, André. 'L'Office du crucifix contre l'angoisse." *Ephemerides Liturgicae*, 46 (1932):421-34.

Wordsworth, Christopher, and Littlehales, Henry. *The Old Service Books of the English Church*. London: Methuen, 1904.

"York Breviary." *Breviarium ad Usum Insignis Ecclesiae Eboracensis*. Edited by Stephen W. Lawley. Surtees Society, 71, 75 (1871-1875).

**Ancrene Riwle**, anonymously set down as an instructional treatise for three well-born anchoresses, is one of the few substantial prose works surviving from the early Middle English period. Written in a graceful style, the work consists of an Introduction followed by eight separate Parts, each dealing with an aspect of the anchoritic life. The Introduction explains the importance of guidelines for the religious life; Part I, which specifies the regimen of daily devotions and directions for liturgical services, is primarily concerned with the anchoresses' spiritual development. Parts II–VII discuss inward matters (control of senses and feelings, temptation, penitence, confession, love of Christ), while Part VIII returns to outward concerns such as rules for eating and drinking.

In the present work, Roger Dahood and the late R. W. Ackerman have edited and translated the Introduction and Part I, basing their text on BL MS Cotton Cleopatra C.VI. Their substantial introduction traces the origins of anchoritic life and shows the relationship of these parts to the whole of **Ancrene Riwle**. The text and translation are supported by textual notes, full annotation of prayers, hymns, and verses, many now identified for the first time. The facing-page translation and the rich notes make the work accessible to general readers as well as to scholars and students.

The late **Robert W. Ackerman** was Professor of English Philology at Stanford University and the author of *Backgrounds of Medieval English Literature* (1966); *Sir Francis Madden: A Biographical Sketch and Bibliography*, with Gretchen P. Ackerman (1979); *Ywain, The Knight of the Lion*, translated with F. W. Locke (1957); and *An Index of the Arthurian Names in Middle English* (1952). **Roger Dahood** is Associate Professor of English at the University of Arizona. He has published a number of articles on Old and Middle English literature and is the editor of the forthcoming *Avowing of King Arthur*.

# mRts

## meðieval & Renaissance texts & stuðies
is the publishing program of the
Center for Medieval & Early Renaissance Studies
at the State University of New York at Binghamton.

mRts emphasizes books that are needed —
texts, translations, and major research tools.

mRts aims to publish the highest quality scholarship
in attractive and durable format at modest cost.